by Cécile

FEMMES FATALES

Femmes Fatales restores to print the best of women's writing in the classic pulp genres of the mid-twentieth century. From mysteries to hard-boiled noir to taboo lesbian romance, these rediscovered queens of pulp offer subversive perspectives on a turbulent era.

Faith Baldwin
SKYSCRAPER

Vera Caspary
BEDELIA
LAURA

Dorothy B. Hughes
THE BLACKBIRDER
IN A LONELY PLACE

Gypsy Rose Lee
THE G-STRING MURDERS
MOTHER FINDS A BODY

Evelyn Piper
BUNNY LAKE IS MISSING

Olive Higgins Prouty
NOW, VOYAGER

Valerie Taylor
THE GIRLS IN 3-B
STRANGER ON LESBOS

Tereska Torrès
WOMEN'S BARRACKS
BY CECILE

by Cécile

TERESKA TORRES

THE FEMINIST PRESS
AT THE CITY UNIVERSITY OF NEW YORK
NEW YORK CITY

Published in 2012 by the Feminist Press
at the City University of New York
The Graduate Center
365 Fifth Avenue, Suite 5406
New York, NY 10016

feministpress.org

First Feminist Press edition

Cover and text design by Drew Stevens.
Cover photo from *Les Liaisons Dangereuses*, 1959. Courtesy of Astor Picture/
Photofest.

Library of Congress Cataloging-in-Publication Data
Torrès, Tereska.
 By Cécile / Tereska Torrès.
    p. cm.
 ISBN 978-1-55861-805-3
1. Young women—France—Fiction. 2. Paris (France—
History—1944—Fiction. 3. Feminist fiction. I. Title.
 PS3570.O7B9 2012
 813'.54—dc23

                              2012028224

by Cécile

PART 1

CÉCILE OPENS HER EYES. IN THE DAWN, HER EYES are gray as the dawn, gray as the dew, gray as the morning fog that stretches itself over the earth, and then rises lightly upward, only to vanish in a few moments with the arrival of the sun.

With the arrival of the sun, Cécile's eyes will no longer be gray. They will turn blue. Of course, her eyes are blue, says Myette, who ought to know. But her friend Anette declares that Cécile's eyes are yellow, yellow as corncobs dried in the sun.

It's dawn again, still another dawn that has been given her. Cécile doesn't budge; her eyes—gray, blue, yellow—are as unblinking as the eyes of a cat. She listens. The garden is barely awakening, under her window; this is the hour when the plants speak and the birds still cry out in their sleep; if one listens well, one may hear the snails gliding along the humid leaves.

And this is hers, hers alone. Cécile always awakens all of a piece, instantaneously; life takes hold of her with open hands, and in a single movement she is sitting up in bed; throwing back her heavy braid with an impatient toss she looks out the window to see what time it is; the rosy ray making only the tiniest rent in the sky is enough for her—it's time. She lifts two long, thin arms toward the low ceiling of her room, stretching her narrow bust, while two small breasts, pointed and hard, rise up beneath her nightgown.

1

In another single moment she now flings her legs out of the bed. Uncovered by her nightgown riding up to her thighs, they might well be the legs of a boy, bronzed, excoriated, with knees as distinctly carved as the features of a face. There is nothing round or soft in these knees, glossy-skinned, all tendons and bones—unusual for a girl. Cécile's legs lash the air like a pair of leather thongs, and she's on her feet on the red flagstone floor, shivering under her nightdress. She is always easily cold—she loves the sun and heat. Quickly, she seizes hold of an old turtle-neck sweater flung over the nearest chair, insinuating herself into it with an undulating movement of her neck, shoulders, and back, like some shivering salamander. Picking up a pair of denim trousers trailing on the floor, she manages, even while sticking one leg after another into the jeans, to get over to her window. Outdoors, the dawn is still gray, and Cécile's eyes are two little dawns of exactly the same shade.

These eyes are quite handy as a subject of conversation—their mysterious changeability has already on many an occasion saved the situation, when the common remark about "an angel passes" was not enough to break an awkward silence and restore some animation to Myette's salon. With an impatient movement, Cécile has thrust the tails of her nightgown into her canvas trousers; spitting on her index finger, she slicks her eyebrows, while with the five spread fingers of her other hand she combs the hair tangled all around her head.

What else does she need? On all fours on the floor, she fishes her espadrilles from under the bed, then she seizes a basket from the table, and a pair of garden shears from the top of her dresser.

With tiger bounds, she descends the stairway. All is still asleep in the house; this is the hour that belongs to her alone. The cat sleeps, rolled into a ball on the rocking chair that doesn't rock, even the birds are still asleep in the trees; the plants sleep in the garden, beneath the dew. Cécile closes the kitchen door gently behind her. Because everything still sleeps, it seems to her suddenly, at this hour alone, that she is bigger, stronger, wiser in her freshly wakened awareness, she is no longer merely a simple gamin of nearly eighteen. This feeling fills her with joy, a special joy grown out of her solitude and freedom; she knows that she belongs to herself, that she is she, that everything awaits her. Everything? What, then? She doesn't know what—the important thing is to be ready. During the day, when she is in the midst of her school friends, or in the village, or in the house, there are too many distractions for her to constantly stay ready. During the day, what awaits her may so easily escape her.

But at dawn, in this solitary silence, in the midst of nature itself, nature all one and single, she can listen, and she can awaken one more day for herself, and tell herself, "I am here, here I am, life, I am ready for everything you want to bring me, oh you marvelous life! All your delights, all your loves, all your tastes and scents and feelings! All, because I am so entirely virgin, and so impatient to live . . ."

Bending over the rosebushes, stooping to the strawberry plants, she fills her basket; from the lettuce leaves she pulls off the snails—they are tinted a beautiful pale yellow like newborn chicks—and she replaces each tenderly on some other leaf, more handy than the lettuce. She licks the dew from a pear, breathes the exhalation of the grass, smiles to the flower buds as to a row of babies.

Something warm has just rubbed against her leg; it's Minou, up at last, come to join her. Cécile lifts her, hugs her to herself, scrutinizing the golden eyes of the cat, unblinking eyes like her own.

Beyond this garden—this fortification—people keep killing each other; the full-grown adults are killing or finishing with their killing of each other. It's the summer of 1944, and the Germans have been driven from Paris, but they still put up their fight, some distance beyond. The youth-time of Cécile has known nothing but war—a rather distant war, it has touched this little village only lightly, but it has laid its hand heavily on her family.

During the last four years she has lived with her godmother, Myette, in this village in Gascony, while her parents have been interned in a prison camp. "They'll come back," her grandmother tells her, and Cécile solemnly nods her head. The adults have stolen her childhood from her—and will they also steal her grownup life?

Cécile looks around her anew, absorbing the garden, the sky—everything that is hers alone, at the dawn of each day.

And it is only when she is at last again replenished with the acidulous scents, with the tangy bitter flavors of macerated grasses and leaves, when she is at last enveloped in the final shreds of fog, when she is already warmed by the first stroke of the sun on her neck, and invaded by peace and joy, that Cécile can again close her eyes—these gray eyes already turning blue, and that will turn to yellow, presently, when the cocks sing out in the deliverance that every morning brings.

END OF SEPTEMBER, 1944. The summer of deliverance, the warm summer's end of that year. School has begun again, and after class Cécile hurries over to her best friend, Anette. Anette always put on her white gloves before going home; she is small and round; her hair is short, but her school uniform is a little longer than the fashion. The fashion at a convent school is always one war behind.

"Oh, I'm so hot!" Anette sighs. "The minute I get home, I'm taking off my stockings." For the convent school requires that gray cotton stockings be worn with the blue sailor dress, the white gloves, and the round felt hat that compose the uniform.

"I—" says Cécile—"I'm taking off my stockings as soon as I'm out, behind the courtyard door."

"That's just like Cécile!" thinks Anette. "Cécile isn't afraid of anything! She's an anarchist, she doesn't care at all what people may think, she does whatever comes into her head."

Anette is desperately envious of Cécile's free ways, and divided in her soul between jealousy, admiration, and rancor.

An entire battalion of right-thinking, well-established, well-organized folk rises up in her to disapprove of her friend, whom she wants so much to resemble. "It's just not done!" Anette pronounces this decisive formula, yet she knows that she is beaten in advance, that Cécile will only laugh and say, "All the better!"

Cécile has an irritating way of looking at her, of gazing at everything with her multicolored eyes, and speaking of the present as though it were already in the past. "You remember, yesterday . . ."

Yesterday is almost today, for Anette, for Louise, for Vincente, it's part of the present time, it isn't a period to be remembered and judged. But Cécile speaks of this unfinished time already with a distance, as though it were something in a fable. She seems to find pleasure in pulling out everyday happenings, as though out of a basket, and spreading them before her friends, like a magician turning everything into a trick—the laughter of Louise, the joke played on Vincente, the quarrels of Anette, are spread out and suddenly relived. "You remember," Cécile says, "when Louise promised us to come to school in silk stockings and when Mlle Mazoyllet—"

Mademoiselle teaches literature, and everyone knows that Cécile adores her. "What's Louise got to do with—" Anette begins, for Cécile leaps from one thought to another with a logic that Anette can never follow. "Come on!" Cécile commands. She hasn't put on her gloves—with her, the gloves are always worn inside her pocket! Behind the carriage entrance she bends over; already she's rolled her stockings down to her shoes, like ankle socks. "I've got an idea—but take off your gloves. Anette, you're ridiculous wearing gloves in the heat— we'll go swimming—but don't say a word to anyone, or else they'll all want to come—let's run to the river."

"But," says Anette, "I don't have a bathing suit."

Cécile raises a thin, disdainful shoulder. "What of it, there's never anyone down there, and besides, it's much more pleasant to swim in your skin."

What nerve she has, that Cécile, and what extraordinary things she knows! Anette has never gone swimming in the nude, but this Parisienne Cécile is afraid of nothing.

Cécile laughs as she runs, her schoolbag flung up atop her head, and steadied with one hand, Bedouin-fashion, as though by instinct. If Anette but knew it—neither has she ever been swimming naked anywhere! But the idea pleases her, and it's just as well to give the impression that she knows all about it, otherwise Anette, with her country-girl timidity, will at once refuse. Besides, Cécile likes to appear more daring, more extravagant than she really is. It's sort of a role to play, and has become second nature with her. She doesn't know how she started this role. Was it her arrival in the village at the beginning of the war, and her appearance at the convent—the only girl from Paris—arousing a murmur of astonishment, of stupefaction that has followed her ever since, her advent creating and maintaining a level of wonder to which she herself must constantly rise? Or is it she herself who has created, for her friends, this exciting personage who is afraid of nothing, who has "read everything" and "seen everything" in Paris, and who thereby is entitled to queen it over these little village girls of Gascony?

Once more Cécile has proposed something shocking, and yet here is Anette following her, as always.

As they run, the sun enters into Cécile and Anette through all their pores; it blinds them and leaves them deaf to the world. Anette puffs and blows. Small, rounded, and dark, she quickly becomes hot, and her sweat runs down her back. Already, she has begun to regret having let herself be dragged along. She tells herself that one shouldn't swim when one is so hot, she'll surely catch pneumonia and die. And besides—to go swimming altogether naked—it must be even more dangerous!

But Cécile gallops along, laughing.

Luckily, the pathway opening before them is filled with shade, pierced only by strands of light like those that play through the windows of a cathedral. The two girls run, their schoolbags bouncing on their heads, while brambles reach out their fingers to stop them, catching hold of their skirts, and letting go only regretfully, detaching themselves with little cracklings of anger.

And as always, Cécile feels as though she were detaching herself from her own person, that she is moving over while another Cécile begins to run alongside her, and today the second Cécile is pursued by bandits—that's why she's running so hard—they want to catch her, they will violate her—hurry! She must flee at all costs!

Cécile throws a hurried look at Anette just behind her. Anette is her maid, following her and carrying the baby—that large, maroon-colored bundle in her arms—the bandits want to kill the baby—the baby is the son of Aga Khan—"Oh, I'm so hot! I'm going to die!" Anette gasps. She lets herself drop to the ground, fat maroon schoolbag tumbling, too, and disgorging books and note papers. Cécile's dream is interrupted, and she too halts, irritated.

"Come on, then! We're nearly there!" Cécile cries. "Don't stop now, when we're only a minute from the river!" But she kneels for a minute alongside Anette, and her eyes, golden in the shade, crinkle with laughter. "I was telling myself a story while I ran, and you've spoiled everything; you interrupted my story!"

"What story? Tell me, while we rest?"

"No, not now—after—tonight . . ." Disappointed, Anette slowly gets up; strands of hair are still pasted to her cheeks; she bends and gathers her books and her note papers. Cécile's stories have woven a tapestry through her life, during the three years of their friendship. There are the stories that Cécile reads—for her godmother lets her read whatever she wants, even the authors forbidden on the Index, like Victor Hugo or Alexandre Dumas. Anette is allowed to read only a few selected works of theirs—expurgated, of course. Mère Stanislas has a predilection for certain stuffy authors like Boileau or Corneille. Three-fourths of French literature is studied without being read—while Cécile, for her part, relates to Anette all sorts of astonishing things that take place in the pages of Baudelaire and Musset, and to which she adds whatever she makes up in her own head—episodes that are even more astonishing! What sort of a story, then, has she just made up?

Anette gathers her schoolbag without realizing that but an instant ago this schoolbag was the illegitimate child of the Aga Khan.

The river is there in the hollow before them, bordered by weeping willows rinsing their hair all along its banks. Not a soul is about—for who would be so crazy as to come under the open sun in this heat?

Without waiting, Cécile flings her bag to the ground, and atop it fall her slippers, her gray stockings, her sailor-blue skirt, and her uniform blouse.

Modest Anette undresses behind a bush, folding her garments one by one as though she were in her room at home.

"Oh! It's so cold!" cries Cécile.

"It's cold?" Anette worries. She emerges from behind her bush, still dressed in her white cotton slip with its eyelet embroidery, and she tests the water with the tips of her toes. Then she kneels at the edge of the clear stream, and splashes her face and neck and arms.

Cécile is already afloat in the midst of the river—she has cast off—she is far away—her braid floats on the water alongside her, like a serpent of the sea—her white naked body is imprinted with trembling shadows from the creepers and branches that line the narrow river and form a green roof above it. Floating like that, Cécile's body has the look of a martyr's tied with ropes and made ready for torture. Or else—is she Ophelia? Ophelia lost, Ophelia mad, Ophelia dead?

But no, she is neither lost nor dead—happiness penetrates her, through every part of her being; she is turned toward the sky, and at this moment happiness, total happiness, is this roof of living green, pierced by hundreds of suns, all the suns that sing! Happiness is the water, so fresh, caressing her shoulders, her back, her thighs, happiness is the transparency of the river and the marvelous enchanted pebbles that scintillate in the river's bed.

How is it possible? Here, this peace, this silence, this overwhelming happiness, and there, the war that is not finished, and hunger, misery, and her parents perhaps under torture, perhaps dead. Paris is still plunged in darkness and cold.

It is unjust, it is monstrous, and how can she alone have the right to be so happy at this moment? Isn't she guilty of a monstrous selfishness?

Cécile begins to feel cold; she shivers, turns over, and swims vigorously toward the shore, presently catching hold of a branch hanging over the river. Anette is still there, her legs in the water, sitting on the bank in her slip, and she looks at Cécile's naked body with a shocked air.

"If someone should see you!" she mutters under her breath, as though she were afraid of attracting some witness by the sound of her voice.

"Coward!" cries Cécile. "It was wonderful! Go, swim in your slip, if you're so scared!"

She stretches out on the grass. Her heart beats wildly, she feels the blood running in her veins like so many little streams through her body; she has become the river, her wet hair is a jungle of creepers and seaweed. Her skin has taken on an animal heat. It is like this that Cécile most loves life—when she can feel herself melted away into nature, when she can taste the sand, the grass, the water, feeling herself intimately and sensually a part of the created world around her.

Anette watches her, taking her silence for sadness. "You still haven't received any word of your parents?" she asks, as she has been asking during the last three years.

"Nothing. But I'm sure they're alive, and now that Paris has been liberated for more than a month—"

"What are you going to do?"

"Go to Paris, of course," says Cécile. "See what has become of our apartment, ask our old friends, the concierge. There must be some organizations, from the Resistance, that might know where they were deported to . . ."

The apartment, the six large rooms, the salon with its windows giving onto the Seine, her mother, whose visage is somehow fading . . . She had been only thirteen the last time—when they had painted the windows blue because of the blackout—her father, sitting in his invalid chair, in his study, and writing . . . She only sees him that way, always writing, composing those mysterious manuscripts that no one had the right to read, not even his wife, the thick manuscripts that he then bound in leather, with his own hands, and on which he engraved his titles in letters of gold. Then he would place his books, one after the other, on the highest shelf in the library. For this father of hers wrote neither for glory, nor for money; he wrote for art's sake alone, pure art.

Paris, before the war . . . a little girl who was an only child . . . the voice of her father, singing, her mother's smile, her scent, the touch of her soft hand, the taste of apricots in the very special tart that she alone knew how to make . . .

During four years, Cécile had been closing her eyes so as to recapture her memories, so as to keep them from escaping her forever . . .

Fortunately there is Myette—what would have become of her without Myette? She sees herself again in 1940, in the arms of Myette while a car carries off her parents, taking them back to Paris, to the occupation, to the Resistance . . .

Myette has never been married; she is about fifty years old, rather fat, but she moves quite lightly. She has the cheeks of a little girl, very rosy and very round, with limpid blue eyes, and curly hair which she twists carelessly into a heavy bun—usually half-undone—that bobs along the back of her neck.

From daybreak, every morning, Cécile can hear Myette addressing herself to the hens that clamber up the wooden steps leading to the garden, and to the neighborhood cats that miaul under her windows, and to the trees in front of the house. Myette speaks to them in all seriousness and with tenderness— in the same voice in which Cécile has heard her talking to the Spanish refugees who, before the war, swarmed over the frontiers all along the Pyrenees and arrived in all the villages and in this village too, stranded, so that when there was nowhere else to put them, they had to be bedded down on straw in the village prison—fortunately always empty. In that period, Myette, as soon as she was up in the morning, and after having twisted up her chignon, fed her cats and her chickens, and watered her plants, would fill every available casserole with well-cooked, steaming provender, and then go off to carry the food to hungry Spaniards.

Cécile was only a little girl on vacation then. Since the beginning of the war, Myette's house, of course, had become successively the refuge for Jews, for members of the Resistance, for Alsatians, for Communists, for all those who were in flight, in danger. Myette talked very little with them of politics, or of the cause of their flight, or of their resistance. But she listened, without ever interrupting the accounts of their troubles; she found clothing for them, she brought them food, and she sought out guides who would take them across the Spanish border— the same guides who had formerly served, from the opposite direction, to bring Spanish refugees into France.

At the side of her godmother, Cécile quickly acquired a taste for nature, but also for danger. Her imagination fed on the secret drama that enveloped the hounded derelicts who spent a night in Myette's house and disappeared.

Alone, from the beginning of her stay, and feeling herself so much a stranger, so different from the little girls of her own age—a Parisienne, the daughter of Resistants, burdened with the secret of her parents' allegiance and the secrets of Myette— she had taken the habit of escaping into the garden, to read, to be by herself. Perched for hours at a time amidst the branches of an ancient fig tree, she read Alexandre Dumas and Jack London, while her fingers became sticky with the syrup of green and black figs. She read through an entire library, in that tree. There were no "children's books" on Myette's shelves. Cécile read Victor Hugo, Tolstoy, Balzac, varying only her choice of fruit with the titles. Thus, *Les Misérables* became confused, in her spirit, with the taste of "kakis," that Japanese fruit with the delicate flavor, also known among the more erudite villagers as persimmons. Balzac came during the apple season, and Tolstoy when the plums were ripe, in their violet skins. The great war of her own days was much farther away, for her, than the retreat from Moscow.

STRETCHED OUT NOW in the grass, alongside the silent Anette, Cécile thinks about the war, and her life during the war. Yes, she has spent these four years peacefully, the Germans have appeared very little here, and the greatest risks she has taken have been limited to listening to the BBC from London, to dreaming of General de Gaulle, to keeping silent about Myette's "visitors." She has lived amidst an abundance of fruit, of vegetables, of eggs, in the warmth of the sun of Gascony; her hair has grown very long down her back, she has become bronzed, and taller—but has she really lived? Except in her imagination—has she lived? Hasn't she remained exactly the same little girl that her parents confided to Myette? Was it right, to be so little mature at seventeen?

There is nothing more difficult than to be honest toward our childhood memories. The child, the young girl that a woman once was, conceals herself so easily behind a screen of clichés. It is so difficult to look back without being engrossed by the glowing images created by our sentimental desire for a perfect past.

Cécile knows this by instinct, and what she wants is to seize her past while it is still almost the present, to examine it fresh-picked, to taste it before it spoils, fades, and becomes discolored. She studies Anette and makes note of her little moue of reproach, or of her embarrassed laugh; she tastes the river in the palm of her hand before the water evaporates.

"What are you thinking about?" asks Anette, who is always made uncomfortable by silence.

"About smells," says Cécile, motionless in the grass.

"You're crazy," says Anette. Then, "What do you mean—about smells?"

"The smells of yesterday, and of today. To begin with, the smell of the convent corridors. There's a special smell for the summer and for the winter. In the winter, at five—not at five o'clock exactly, but at what the five o'clock period represents, that is—the classes are finished, the afternoon snack is over, and there are the rows of us going upstairs again from the recreation hall. We're supposed to go and study, and then the corridors smell of disinfectant, and the electric lights make the floors glitter like mirrors, and we're wearing the house slippers that we have to wear instead of shoes, inside the convent, so all the girls seem to be gliding—skating instead of walking . . ."

The girls are just coming from their afternoon snack, so the odor of café au lait and of chicory is still mingled, in Cécile's nostrils, with the odor of disinfectant. The café au lait is steaming in the porcelain bowls that are held in her two hands. No coffee in the world will ever taste as good as this coffee of her adolescence . . . And then, there are the "sacred" odors, the scents of the chapel, the sweet odor of lilies of the field, the sharp odor of the holy water, the heavy odor of incense, and with all this, the odor of the garments of the nuns—an odor clean and dry.

This makes Cécile think of Vincente, who is the only person whose odor has ever made her uncomfortable. Vincente has an acid, disagreeable odor. Stretched in the grass at river's edge, Cécile wrinkles her nose in disgust. "Vincente smells like a hare," Cécile suddenly remarks, and Anette contracts her brows. "It's not nice of you to say that." "It's true," says Cécile. "You're right to say that it's not nice, but it's true, admit it, isn't it true?"

"Don't you like Vincente?" asks Anette.

"But of course, I like her fine, only I don't like her smell—that doesn't prevent me from being fond of her."

Anette can't quite manage to understand this. Everything is always more simple for her. She is irritated by imperfections only in people she doesn't like. The critical spirit of Cécile disorients her.

To change the subject, she pulls nearer to Cécile. "Listen, but you won't tell a soul—you promise me? With you, one never knows." "Oh!" cries Cécile indignantly, "I've never in my life betrayed a secret! You know that perfectly well!"

"All right then, I'll tell you—" and Anette blushes. "You know Antoine, the son of the pharmacist, you know who I mean . . . yesterday, after class, I met him in the street, and we went for a walk, as far as the ramparts, and then, at the Fountain of

Diana, in those little black streets where there's never anyone—he kissed me. He kissed me on the mouth."

Anette's face, as she offers this confidence—Cécile scrutinizes it carefully, like some lock with a secret combination. What is revealed, in this face, beyond what has been said? A sensuality mingled with shame, yet also with pride—but nothing of love, nevertheless, neither in the dark eyes, that are laughing, not in the red, red mouth. Quite lengthily, Anette now describes the technique of the kiss, the time, and the place. Of Antoine, she says nothing. Cécile, who was just about to ask, "Do you love him?" bites her lips and keeps silent.

A first kiss—she imagines it with so much more solemnity—but can one solemnly kiss a pimply boy of nineteen, whose thick fists hang lumpishly out of coat sleeves that are always too short, and whose badly shaved face is always covered with a grayish shadow?

Feeling suddenly chilly, Cécile seizes her slip, her panties, her skirt, dressing hurriedly. It seems to her that Anette has spoiled her afternoon. It was good in the water, in the grass under the sun. Why did she need to talk in such detail about that kiss? Still, all the girls kiss boys—it's normal. "So then he said," continues Anette, "'We'll meet again tomorrow—come at four o'clock, behind Mlle Bertha's shop,' and he laughed, and he said, 'Give me another one, you kiss well for a beginner!'"

"And—you're going?" asks Cécile. It seems incredible to her that Anette, who doesn't love Antoine, lets herself be kissed, and will go running to their rendezvous tomorrow, and that she talks about it in such a tone.

But it is human nature, that's what it is—this strange thing called "human nature" which is the answer to all the puzzling sides of adult life.

While they walk slowly back through the heat, back toward home, Cécile is silent again. And coming into her silence, Anette takes form now with her womanly knowing smile and her eyes clouded and her lips partly open. She is walking with a man, not with Antoine this time, with a man, and they are walking in the streets of Paris. Perhaps Anette is a mistress.

She has on an elegant dress, and her hair is piled high on her forehead, she wears shoes with heels, the man raises his hand to call a taxi . . .

Cécile is dreaming again and Anette is the heroine of a new story, but this story makes her feel sad. Something awful is going to happen to Anette. Is it her own invented tale that brings tears to Cécile's eyes? But that's silly, silly—

Cécile virtually jumps out of her dream. She pulls Anette by the hand, she laughs suddenly, she makes Anette race her to the village.

Anette so loves this bursting laughter of Cécile's.

ANETTE IS ALREADY "going steady" with Antoine. All the girls are going steady with their boys this year, Louise and Vincente and all the rest.

At recess, they gather in their little groups, they troop together. Behind their hands, they choke with smothered laughter. "Well then, our fine Parisienne—what about you—tell us!"

Cécile adopts a mysterious air, and tells them, "It's none of your affair, and besides, he's not just some kid, this one—this is a man, you wouldn't understand."

Now that Paris has been liberated the entire village has learned that over these four years Myette has been hiding people in her house, Jews, parachutists, Resistance fighters—so that Cécile only has an embarrassment of choice in selecting, among these wayfarers of a single night, a lover worthy of her status.

"Who is it? Who are you talking about?" the girls exclaim, rolling their r's in the manner of Gascony. "An Englishman? Tell us, Cécile!"

CÉCILE BURSTS OUT laughing, and runs off to the other end of the courtyard. She climbs up a tree, agile as a cat, and from here she makes faces at her friends, while she starts to sing—

J'ai deux amours
Mon pays et Paris—

Mère Stanislas, espying her from afar, comes running as fast as her long skirts will permit, and commands her, with the sternest of airs, to come down. Cécile is obliged to give ear to a lengthy discourse on young girls of good family, and what is done and what is not done. The rosary of Mère Stanislas clicks with an irritating rattle, Cécile raises her forehead and makes an impertinent reply; from the depths of her skirt Mère Stanislas extracts her little record book, noting several bad points for Cécile, whose reputation is thereby instantly saved: marked wicked and mischievous, she passes before her group of friends, wearing the glorious halo of the incorrigible, the arrogant, of those who are afraid of nothing.

Later, sitting in the empty classroom, Cécile copies a chapter from her history book three times over—a reasonable punishment, she finds, since she is at the same time learning today's lesson. The third time, she can even make her copy without paying attention to the words, so that her thoughts are free to roam elsewhere . . .

If Myette would let her leave . . . but Myette says that the war is still too close to Paris, and that Cécile's parents have placed her here in her care—"Wait a little more, my dear, you've waited four years, wait a few weeks longer . . ." How can one disobey so gentle a voice? How can one go against the boundless goodness of Myette? Myette, who has such a high idea of Cécile's innumerable qualities; Myette who admires and adores her with a spinster's passion.

All the girls of her own age spend their time hunting for flirtations, Cécile reflects, but that is because they have nothing to love. They live alongside their parents, but not *with* them, they don't know them, and they don't let themselves be known by them. For herself everything is different. She has Myette, she has parents whom she adores and who are both heroes, and she has Mlle Mazoyllet; that is quite enough for a girl her age! She has no need of reassurance through flirting with boys.

And for love, she has the flowers, the river, the cat, the dawn. Why should one practice love on the skin of boys, when one may caress a flower, or kiss the leaves of grass, or place one's cheek against the earth still humid with dew and smelling of sap?

"Punished, my little girl?" asks the voice of Mademoiselle behind her. Cécile raises her eyes toward the youthful face that smiles to her.

Mademoiselle smells good—she must use perfume, there is always a scent of lavender hovering about her. Mademoiselle is blond, she has blue eyes and pink skin. The evil tongues of the village even accuse her of having an English ancestor, for in this area there are numbers of people who haven't yet had time, after centuries of habitude, to arrive at the idea that it is no longer England that is the enemy but—since 1870—Germany.

"What have you done now, my little girl?" asks Mademoiselle, in a tone of reproach. It is whispered that Mademoiselle would like to take her vows, but that she has been unable to, because of her delicate health. Cécile lives in constant dread of seeing Mademoiselle either dying, or taking the veil, before her eyes. It seems to her that the delicate frailty of Mademoiselle leaves her no other alternative.

Mademoiselle places her white hand on Cécile's shoulder and Cécile feels herself becoming a river of joy; joy streams all through her body, bubbles in her veins, like the little joyful springs that bubble and jump in the mountains. It is enough for her to feel this hand, she would kiss the palm—but the mere idea alone covers her with a blush of shame.

"I haven't done anything," she says, to give herself dignity. "I had climbed into a tree, and Mère Stanislas ordered me to come down, and gave me a lecture. I detest her!"

Mlle Mazoyllet wrinkles her brow. "You must not speak like that. It's bad to detest anyone, and Mère Stanislas wants nothing—"

"Oh, I know," says Cécile. "She wants nothing but what is good for me, she wants me to conduct myself like a well-brought-up young girl—" Instinctively, Cécile imitates the voice of Mère Stanislas—so exactly, as she repeats her words, that Mademoiselle begins to laugh.

"Cécile, with you—either you detest or you adore, right off!

You're so impassioned! Can't you sometimes feel things a little less violently? And here I've come to ask you to recite a poem for the saint's day of Reverend Mère Clemence—but I think you had a little trouble with her too last week?"

"Oh, but this week I've forgiven her!" says Cécile, who is always ready to recite poetry, to act in plays, to dance and to sing. "What poem were you thinking of, Mademoiselle? Will we have no school on her saint's day?"

Reverend Mère Clemence is the most frequently detested of all the authorities in Cécile's world, and it is in imitating her that Cécile achieves her greatest successes before her little circle of friends. "The Reverend Mère Clemence and her Discourse on the Duties that Await Us in Life," or, even better, "The Reverend Mère Clemence, on the Dangers of the Cinema, the Dance, and Cigarettes."

"What a child you still are, my little one!" says Mlle Mazoyllet, smiling. There is no reproach in her smile, but Cécile nods her head, for she knows that Mademoiselle is right. It's true that she is too infantile, it's true that she is nearly eighteen, that this is her last year in school, that she should be serious and tormented at her age, that she should be thinking of the future, thinking of the war, and that she should perhaps never laugh until her parents are found again. She is always reproaching herself for being too impulsive, too gay, too romantic, too childish altogether, and so little prepared for life. But life frightens her, and she cannot admit this to all these people who think her so gay, so carefree . . .

She is afraid of what awaits her, of the future in a world almost entirely destroyed, in the still-smoking cities where she will perhaps never find her parents. It is so much easier to forget, in laughter, in running to the river, in becoming absorbed in the garden, in Myette, in Myette's chickens and the cats and dogs, or in composing poems of love, in her heart, to Mlle Mazoyllet—

"You're sad?" asks Mademoiselle. "Have I saddened you, Cécile? I didn't mean to. It's good to remain a child a while longer, you have time enough to become an adult."

It is the voice of Mlle Mazoyllet that becomes saddened now. Instantly, Cécile forgets her pain, in her worry over the pain she divines in the voice of the one she so loves. What made Mademoiselle say that? Had she herself become adult too soon? Had she suffered, at too early an age? Cécile feels ready to kill whoever it was, man or woman, that brought suffering to Mademoiselle.

But her adored one only responds, "What of the poem, then, Cécile? Do you have an idea? You who read so much— do you have a favorite poem that might be appropriate for this occasion?"

Mademoiselle teaches literature at Cécile's class at the convent, and they have had long private discussions on the books Cécile has been reading. "Oh!" cries Cécile, "I've just read some poems—the most beautiful book of poems I've ever read!"

Mademoiselle laughs gently over her pupil's enthusiasm. "*Les Chansons de Bilitis!*" says Cécile. "have you read them, Mademoiselle?"

Mademoiselle reddens a bit. "Good heavens, Cécile, I hope you're not thinking for an instant of reading *Les Chansons de Bilitis* before the Reverend Mère Clemence! Good heavens, she would faint!"

Cécile begins to laugh. "I know," she says, "I know it would be impossible, even though, truly, the songs are very pure, Mademoiselle, and very beautiful. You like them, don't you?... No, for Reverend Mère Clemence I'll recite—" and Cécile mounts a chair and begins to recite, in a lugubrious voice:

Je suis un berceau
qu'une main balance
au creux d'un caveau.
Silence! Silence!

And leaping from the chair, she adds, "Verlaine," while bowing to an imaginary audience. At the same instant, in quite another voice, she continues:

Il m'a dit 'Cette nuit j'ai rêvé,
J'avais ta chevelure autour de mon cou—
J'avais tes cheveux comme un collier noir
Autout de ma nuque et sur ma poitrine—

Mlle Mazoyllet watches the changeable eyes, blue, green, golden, lifted toward her, and she speaks the rest of the poem of Pierre Louÿs, together with Cécile—

Je les caressais et c'étaient les miens
Et nous étions liées pour toujours ainsi—

But the door opens, and Cécile breaks off, at the same time as Mademoiselle.

It is only the sister doorkeeper, in search of Mère Stanislas; she shuts the classroom door again.

"See what you made me do, Cécile, you're going to have me dismissed! *Les Chansons de Bilitis* are not to be recited in a school for young ladies! Come now, we'd better think seriously about Reverend Mère Clemence. What about a passage from Esther?"

Cécile makes a moue. "Oh! Always and eternally Racine or Corneille!"

"'The Lake,' then?" proposes Mademoiselle. Cécile sighs. "Oh, that, you can be sure she'll love that!" and her voice immediately takes on the tone of the Mother Superior. "You have just heard a recitation by one of your young friends of one of the most moving poems in the whole of French literature. I hope that you have all experienced the profound Christian inspiration that alone can render a work of art worthy of that designation."

In the distance, a bell sounds. It is the bell that regulates the life of the convent, heavily ringing out the hours of awakening, of meals, of classes, of recitation, and of sleep.

The little sister from the kitchen must be hanging onto the long chain, her face all red, framed in her bonnet with its black and white piping, her sleeves rolled up to her elbows to enable her to pull more forcefully.

Cécile listens to the bell with that air of concentration that never fails to astonish Mademoiselle. What can this child really be listening to like that? What is it that she looks at, with her intensity?

And Cécile repeats, within herself, "And the bell, too, I must remember it, the bell, and the sister cook, and the odor of the school at five o'clock, and the smile of Mademoiselle, and her frightened air when I mentioned *Les Chansons de Bilitis*, I must remember, I must never forget the courtyard of the school, and the girls, and the fog, the sun, the gardener's black dog, and Anette's white cat, the mornings and the evenings . . . But what use will it be for me to remember all this if I can never manage to become an adult?"

"What are you thinking of, Cécile?" asks Mlle Mazoyllet.

Cécile shakes herself and begins to laugh. "Of nothing," she says.

MYETTE IS HOLDING the letter in her hand when Cécile comes from school.

What at once astonishes Cécile is to see Myette awaiting her with a letter, rather than with a pot of jam or a bowl filled with fruit.

In the four years that Cécile has been coming home to this house, Myette has always been there like some distracted mother cat, almost running to their encounter, smoothing Cécile's hair, sniffing her, seeming to want to efface from the features, from the hair of her godchild every trace of the hours that have been passed away from herself. Before Cécile can say a word, she has always had to drink a glass of currant juice that Myette has concocted, or taste the pears, or the strawberries from the garden, or the jelly, still warm, just made this afternoon . . .

Only then will Myette, reassured, draw the girl down onto her lap in the great wicker armchair, and demand, "Now tell me, my fine beauty, what have you done today?"

But this afternoon Myette holds nothing in her hand but the sheet of white paper, on which there runs a writing so miniscule that one might think that there are only light, delicate lines traced across the page, lines that do not form letters, only a series of sea-blue threads marking undulating wavelets on a deserted beach.

It is a serious face that Myette presents to Cécile, but seeing the inquietude awakened in her godchild, she cries out at once, "No, no, my darling, it's not bad news, not for you—only for me perhaps . . . but where is my head! I haven't fixed anything for you to eat! Wait!" And she dashes at once toward her kitchen, with Cécile following her.

"But what is it, Godmamma? From whom is this letter? Oh, nougat! Where on earth did you get the nougat, Godmamma?"

"Eat it! It's for you! And just do me the favor of tasting this apple! Isn't it beautiful! Look at the color on it! Mlle Angelique brought me a basketful!"

"Mlle Angelique! Just what does she want to know now, if she's bringing you gifts of apples, Godmamma? That stingy old crow, I'll bet she's complaining about me again!"

Myette laughs and becomes angry at the same time. "Cécile! Don't talk like that! She's a poor old woman, very lonely!"

But Myette knows that Cécile is right, that the old maid is stingy and evil-minded, and that she turns up at the slightest opportunity to murmur in her unctuous little voice, "Your Cécile—I saw her running again, right in the middle of the street, and without her hat, and without gloves! You permit her everything, it's not right, she'll turn bad, she has no respect for anyone, a young girl of her age should stop politely and say good day, and she shouldn't talk in such a loud voice, or laugh so much, it just isn't done . . . perhaps in Paris, but here in the country, thank God, it isn't done!"

"No, Cécile," Myette says, "Mlle Angelique is not bad, she's just full of curiosity, and lonely, and she has nothing to do with herself, so when she saw the postman bringing me a letter—special delivery and registered—naturally she wanted to know—"

"Then what about the letter?" Cécile asks, in her turn.

"Well—it concerns you—it concerns your parents too, but this does not bring news of them yet. Do you know, do you remember—someone named Maurice Henry?"

"Maurice Henry?" Cécile repeats. She has no memory of this name. No face emerges to her from the shadows.

"A friend of your father's," Myette insists. Cécile closes her eyes. How difficult it is for her to call them up, or even see herself again as she was; all the friends of her parents, too, have vanished into the fog of her childhood. She shakes her head.

"He was in the Resistance with your parents. You parents were deported, my dear, but they are surely alive, they'll come back, now that Paris has been liberated, the war won't last much longer. The gentleman writes that he has only now, at last, found my address, and he thinks that you should come to Paris. Your parents' apartment is unoccupied, and if you don't go there it will be requisitioned, and since all your father's papers are there, his manuscripts, his books, someone ought to take care of it—"

Myette holds out the letter to Cécile, and turns away her head so as not to show her tears. The day has come, the day she feared so much, when Cécile would have to leave her. And Cécile mutely bends her head over the sheet of paper, over the microscopic handwriting, deciphering her name, here and there, inscribed by an unknown hand. The very letters seem to call to her, "Cécile . . . Cécile . . . Cécile . . ."

THAT CÉCILE IS but a child, Myette, of course, knows quite well. But isn't this normal enough? What need has she already to become a woman? Life will seize hold of her soon enough, and with her sensual and passionate temperament, life will be difficult enough, too!

Going to her kitchen window, Myette looks out smilingly upon the figure of Cécile perched in her fig tree, her hair undone, streaming over her shoulders, while, absorbed in a book, she bites into her apple—a familiar picture, for the last four years.

How much she resembles her father—she has the same eyes, sometimes golden, sometimes gray-green, the same mouth with its fine delicate lips, so quick to tauten, so quick to tremble with chagrin or laughter—a delicate, an infantile mouth. Myette had spent her childhood with Cécile's father, who was her cousin. And if she had been in love with him, she never told anyone.

He was an artistic soul, and it was in Paris that he had to live. After the war of 1914, invalided on a veteran's pension, he had married Cécile's mother, and dedicated his life to writing. It is from him that Cécile has inherited her imagination, her gift for play-acting, for singing and dancing. Myette's memories are rich with the good childhood days with her cousin who organized plays in the barn, and who told such wonderful stories.

Would he ever return from the present war? What need had there been for him, invalid as he was, to get mixed up with the Resistance? Yet it had been unthinkable that he would not get into it. He had always been of a piece, an enthusiast, courageous—exactly as Cécile is, too. Yes, she must let Cécile depart. Today. She must tell her that what awaits her now will be war, and solitude, and above all, life—a life for which Myette has in no way prepared her. Has she been wrong? Should she send some warning to this Maurice Henry? "Monsieur, I send you the daughter of our friend Royer. She is seventeen. She is still a child—I have kept her close to me for four years, and she knows nothing beyond nature, and poetry, and childish friendships, she believes in everything, she is not ready—"

But ready for what? Is Myette herself much more ready, at fifty? Does she know life any better than Cécile? Is she not herself but a provincial old maid? Should she not write to him, then, "If ever you find that Cécile's parents have been killed, as all signs would lead us to believe, then I beg you, be good enough to my little Cécile to send her back to me, she will need me, she has never yet suffered—"

No, Myette can write nothing to Maurice Henry; she does not even know who he is. She knows only that this child perched in the tree must come down, and must depart.

MAURICE HENRY . . . Seated in the train, she rereads his letter, this letter that speaks of the war, the Resistance, the deportation of her parents. "We have no news of them, but this in itself tells us absolutely nothing. The camps in Germany will soon be liberated—" Meanwhile, Cécile must come to Paris as quickly as possible; if not, the apartment will be requisitioned, her father has left all his papers, his manuscripts—someone must take care of all of this—

Yes, Cécile will show him that she may be counted on. She will take care of everything, like a woman. She has too long been held aside from this war; now she has left Cécile-the-child in the arms of Myette, and it is another Cécile, an adult Cécile, who is on the way to Paris, and this Cécile rereads the letter on the train, contracting her brows over the curious handwriting, so strangely miniscule.

In the bespattered washroom of the train, she rolls up her long braid—thick as her arm—coiling the hair atop her head, trying to find a coiffure that will give her a bit more age. In her handbag, Cécile has hidden a lipstick borrowed from Louise, and now she attempts a makeup. In secrecy from Myette, she has undone the hem of one of her skirts, and in the washroom she changes, putting on for the remainder of the voyage a tight skirt that comes down nearly to her ankles.

Satisfied, Cécile examines herself in the mirror above the washbasin. The mirror is as filthy as the rest of the place, so grimy that she can scarcely recognize herself in the grayish face peering out at her. This is really already another Cécile, with painted lips, and with that crumbling pyramid of golden hair atop her head.

Above all, she must not disappoint him; she must not appear provincial or infantile, she repeats to herself, contracting her brows, folding her lips together.

And the train, after interminable hours and hours, with continual halts in the midst of empty fields, at last arrives, emitting sighs and groans of fatigue, in the city of Paris, which Cécile had left in 1940.

It is December of 1944, and Cécile had forgotten that it could be so cold, so gray—the rain hurls itself against the windows of the railway car, the platform is filled with soldiers, with refugees, everything smells of war and fog. All at once the entire war comes down upon her like a black cape falling on her shoulders and covering her entirely, annihilating her.

She stands on the platform, valise in hand, in the din of the station, enveloped in smoke, suffocated by that bitter odor of large cities that she had forgotten. Almost the entire crowd presses past her side, the mass of soldiers, the crowd of repatriates, women with their children coming from the zone that has just been liberated, Parisians who had fled and who now at last may return home; she has remained alone, standing there, repeating to herself with a despair that she has never known, "My parents too will return like this, like all these repatriates, I'll wait for them now in Paris." She clutches the valise, she shivers, it seems to her that she is the only one on the platform now. And what will she do if Maurice Henry doesn't come? Only five minutes ago she had been telling herself how adult she must be, how she must impress him as much by all her knowledge as by her maturity, and already she feels herself as frightened as a child of four lost at a fair.

Then she hears her name called, just near her, "Cécile?" and the joy that floods her is so strong that if she dared she would throw herself on his neck. He is there, she is no longer lost, this is a friend of her parents, she is saved. She looks at him, laughing with joy, and he looks at her with an air at once satisfied and astonished.

He does not look at all like his handwriting. She had expected an old man, as meticulous as his minute, tight handwriting. But the man who studies her is quite robust; he looks to be about forty years old, but despite this age, which seems extremely advanced to Cécile, he doesn't have the air of an old man. He has the look of an artist—he wears a black, fringe-style beard, a Canadian storm jacket with a fur collar, and a Scotch-plaid scarf is wound around his neck, with its end flapping behind him in the wind of the open platform. He has piercing eyes, a very red mouth; he has the air of a bull, and his voice, too, is very low and strong.

"Well, well," he says, "here I was, coming to meet a child, a little girl, I almost brought a doll along with me to greet you, but I should have brought a bouquet of flowers! It's a ravishing young lady that I find! What a wonderful surprise!"

As Cécile extends her hand to him, he bends, his mouth is warm on Cécile's hand, and it lingers.

"But this changes everything," he repeats, "this changes everything, I shall reorganize all my plans!" Cécile smiles, amused, not understanding what there may be to reorganize, but flattered at being so admired. For Maurice Henry doesn't take his eyes from her. "You resemble your father," he says, "but still—you have your mother's magnificent hair. And what a color! Let me have a good look at you." He looks, and Cécile blushes. He has such a way of looking!

To remain on her dignity, Cécile returns Maurice's stare for stare—yes, he has a refined elegance, the sort of elegance that doesn't exist in Gascony. Even M. Edouard, the handsomest man of the little village, the banker's son, with his terrible reputation of being a dreadful Don Juan—even he doesn't dress like Maurice Henry. That scarf, carelessly thrown around the throat, that beard, that fur collar, the breadth of his shoulders, the sport shoes—everything is pleasing to Cécile, and this must be quite apparent, for Maurice asks, "Well, then—I too pass the inspection? It's all right? We'll be friends, I can say *tu* to you?"

Should she perhaps not have looked at him in the same way that he looked at her? Is it perhaps not done? But she's a little country savage, she doesn't have any idea of what is done or not done in Paris. And besides, she is so happy to have found him and not to be any longer alone in Paris! By his simple presence, Maurice Henry has swept away the fog, the cold, the sadness. "Come on," says Cécile, suddenly happy and filled with hope. She puts her hand through Maurice's arm, as she has seen the stars do in the movies. The women always have their hands through the arms of the men who escort them, and she is a woman now, that's decided.

"Come on, I want to see Paris, and besides, I'm dying of hunger."

"Ah! I see that we're going to understand each other!" cries

Maurice. "I'm hungry too—so hungry that I could eat you up!"
Cécile laughs. "Ah, then it's you—the wolf?" she asks.

"Yes," says Maurice. "The wolf—it is I."

In front of the station, a jeep awaits them.

"I HAVE DISCOVERED something sensational!" announces Maurice. "You simply cannot imagine it—an adorable girl, ravishing, amusing, more fresh than anything I've seen in the last twenty years, a slender, supple body, small breasts, a lovely mouth, hair that falls all the way to her hips, a gift of mimicry, of storytelling! I had dinner with her last night and I haven't been so amused since the beginning of the war. I even think I'm in love."

The painter, sitting opposite Maurice on the terrace of the Deux Magots, raises his shoulders. "You'll get over it, Maurice. You told me almost exactly the same words last month about a WAC in the American army."

"I?" cries Maurice, indignantly. "That WAC? What WAC? I don't even remember her, that was nothing compared to Cécile, and besides, with this Cécile, I'm in a way her guardian, she's the daughter of some friends of mine who were deported— Royer's daughter—you must have heard of him, he worked with me on that underground newspaper in 1941, '42 . . . No, Cécile is different, completely different—you'll see her—I'm going to bring her tonight to the Marchands'." Maurice gets up, making a sign to the waiter. "Leave it," says the painter, "I'll take care of it."

"Okay, old man, until tomorrow night, and don't forget to write the review of that exposition, I need it for my paper no later than Thursday."

Flinging his scarf around his neck, Maurice goes off with a rapid step. He's in a hurry. He is always in a hurry. He promised Cécile to come by for her at four, he still has to go to his paper, and see Henriette, and telephone that British army captain, a scenario writer in civilian life, who has, it seems, a fantastic subject for a film . . .

Meanwhile Maurice hurries down the rue de Rennes with long strides.

Toward him, there advances a brunette, highly made up, quite pretty, in a very short red dress with very high heels. Maurice throws a single glance her way, a professional of course. The girl comes toward him smiling—she has a smile of absolute indecency. How does she do it? Is it that tip of her pointed tongue, between her lips? Accompanied by an oscillation of her highly pointed breasts, sure to be naked under that tight red dress? Maurice slows down, to the devil with Henriette, with the captain, the paper will come out late—this girl amuses him. She has halted, in front of him. Her eyes are unbelievably smutty—you would say they were two tiny film screens showing filthy movies.

"Are you coming with me, *chéri*?" she says; the voice too is lascivious; she has a special tone, for uttering the banal phrase.

"Where to?" asks Maurice.

"To my place," she says. "Very near here."

"For how much?" says Maurice.

"That depends on what you want, *chéri*."

Five minutes of negotiations on the sidewalk. Maurice has a fertile imagination, and he knows how to bargain. The girl is more and more provocative, her eyes, her lips, her breasts are all in the line of combat and obey her like well-trained soldiers. Finally Maurice comes down to an agreement on the price and the merchandise to be delivered.

"Come on then to my place," says the girl. Maurice starts off. But something rings a bell in him—what is it? He can't quite tell at once—but something is out of order. Ah! But of course, it's the voice. The way in which she said, "Come on then to my place." The voice had totally changed. The whole lascivious quality of a moment ago had been emptied from it. She had suddenly spoken in a voice that was bored, tired, detached. Maurice examines the girl, and all at once the entire face, beside him, is as altered as the voice. The mouth is no more than a lipstick mouth badly put on, the eyes have gone out, the breasts are no longer pointed under the dress but seem to be falling. Once the bargaining is over, the girl is only in a hurry to finish with the job as quickly as possible, she is deflated in one stroke like a balloon; she has put away her display for the next client, like a street merchant who puts away his merchandise in a suitcase, until the next pitch where he must spread it out again. "Good Lord!" thinks Maurice—"to lose my time for that!" hastily, he pulls a bill from his pocket, thrusts it into the girl's hand. "Excuse me, I've just remembered a meeting that had completely slipped my mind—I'll come back tomorrow," and before the girl has had time to open her mouth, Maurice signals a taxi and jumps inside. In the cab, he begins to laugh. What a story! He'll tell it to Cécile. Cécile? Can he tell it to her? Why not? Cécile is no prude, one can talk about everything to her. It will amuse her. Besides, it is a good scene to use in that next novel, he'll tell his collaborator, he mustn't forget . . .

Maurice takes out a cigar, lights it. Cécile has only been in Paris for two days, but he feels himself younger by ten years. "I wonder whether she's a virgin—that little one," he asks himself. "Certainly, yes. No. Certainly, no."

There is something special in Cécile that Maurice has difficulty in understanding, and his failure to understand attracts him all the more. The boring thing about most women is that one knows everything right off. They are too simple for Maurice and too easy. They let themselves be taken by him as quickly as that girl on the sidewalk. These modern women think themselves so highly developed, they have become so intoxicated with their liberty and their equality, that they fail to realize they have lost all interest for a man like Maurice. The women all walk around advertising their taste for things sexual, and their lack of inhibition. There is no longer a great difference between them and that girl of a moment ago—except that this one in the end would have cost a great deal less. One doesn't have to take her out, take her to dinner, buy her flowers, one isn't obliged to waste one's time in her company.

Cécile doesn't have that free air about her—yet she has a licentious mouth—and eyes that are pure. This combination is intriguing. She blushes, and at the same time she starts to laugh with the laughter of a complete woman. She has the air of someone disguised at the same time as a woman and an innocent girl. Everything about her disorients Maurice, and he is irritated at thinking too much about her, during the two days that she has been there.

AGAIN, THE ELECTRICITY is off. It happens twenty times a day. Cécile has become used to it, just as she has become habituated to the gray bread, the cold water, the freezing apartment.

Just now, Maurice telephones.

As soon as she hears his voice, Cécile feels herself blushing. This annoys her. She doesn't understand herself. When Maurice is not there, she awaits him; the moment he arrives, she senses that she is afraid of him. She doesn't understand why she fears him—he is comical, he jokes, he amuses her, he fascinates her, he treats her like a woman.

"I'll come for you in half an hour," he just said. "Tomorrow is Christmas, we'll have a real Christmas supper. Our last Christmas of the war."

She waits for him in the apartment, while the darkness comes down little by little. It is only a week that she has been in Paris—a strange week, the strangest of her life.

Cécile raises her head. She stands before her father's library shelves, and up there, on the highest shelf, is that row of forbidden books, the novels written by her father when she was a little girl, the novels that no one had the right to read.

Now too, Cécile does not feel she has the right to touch them. Alone in the dark icy apartment, Cécile gazes up, and her eyes move from one end to the other, over the dozen volumes which her father himself bound in leather. She can barely make out the titles, whose gilded letters shine like glowworms in the shadows. These titles, which her father engraved with his own hand—what dreams, what romances, what tales, what sacred memories are hidden behind them, in the manuscript pages up there? Is there, in all those pages, an answer to the questions Cécile asks herself?

In one week, it seems to her that her entire life has been totally changed. For Maurice Henry has pulled her at once into the astonishing confusion of his own existence. Maurice is at one and the same time, it seems, a critic of art, of the theater, of music, as well as a novelist, a dramatist, a journalist, and a Parisian celebrity on his own, just like Maurice Chevalier or Mistinguette.

Exactly what he did in the Resistance, Cécile cannot quite understand. It seems that he edited some underground newspapers, together with Cécile's father. The two of them together would write these papers, and distribute them—as well as brochures, and posters, and appeals. A whole group of young people were their aides, writing at night, in cellars, and distributing the papers at dawn while the city still slept.

With Maurice, Cécile, in the course of a single week, has discovered what four years of war were like. But this war consists not only of the Resistance, the Maquis, the Germans, it consists also of the cafés of St. Germain-des-Prés, where Maurice takes her, and where the discussion of art, of literature, of philosophy, last the whole night. There, odd men who have the air of women sit opposite odd young women who have the air of boys.

Installed in elegant apartments in Passy, there are black market restaurants, where Maurice has her served with thick, juicy steaks such as one has not even seen in Gascony for four years. On the table are huge blocks of butter, and platters of cheeses. The proprietor speaks with a Russian accent. A young man with long hair and tight American blue jeans recites incomprehensible poems of his own composition. A girl with long hair loose on her shoulders gets up to sing in a hoarse voice. And Cécile above all compels herself not to show her surprise or ignorance in front of the sophisticated and brilliant Maurice.

For his opinion of her has begun to count terribly much. For the sake of his view of her, Cécile forces herself always to appear droll and gay—so that she may see flickering in Maurice's somber eyes, that little glitter of amusement that flatters her.

She knows in advance how it will be when they go out

together tonight. First there will be an elaborate dinner in some black market restaurant, with a great many friends crowded around Maurice, for since his arrival for her at the station she has never seen him alone, Maurice lives only in a crowd. He will be surrounded by girls and boys, most of them in uniform, uniforms of liberated France, uniforms of the Resistance, American uniforms, English, Polish, Belgian, Czech, war correspondents, medical men, aviators. And there will be those too young for the armed forces, in their own uniform, the *zazous* who have sprung up since the liberation, with their long hair, their close-fitting pants, their raucous voices.

At this same hour, down there in Myette's country, everyone is getting ready for the midnight mass. Even during the war, everyone kept up with the custom of the paper lanterns, walking with them to the cathedral, and the blessed loaves that would be distributed after the third Mass, and there were the sheep, the donkeys, and the cattle that were to be blessed on this Christmas night. There had been no Christmas gifts during the war—except that Myette would prepare a wonderful supper, and under her napkin Cécile would find the most beautiful flower of the garden, with an embroidered handkerchief or a book.

It's freezing outdoors. The streets are being patrolled because of German parachutists who have recently come down from behind the front lines. Cécile gets up and goes to the window. Beyond the windows, still painted blue and crisscrossed with adhesive paper, she can make out the city plunged in night. And beyond that is war, scarcely a few hours away; only a number of kilometers away there are soldiers and battlefields, shells bursting, and still further, just a little bit further on, there are the prisoners and the deportees in the camps which are spoken of, in Paris, only in lowered voices—the camps where the living skeletons still breathe, but scarcely. And two of these skeletons, perhaps . . .

And then, there are all the cities in ruins, ruins such as have never been seen before.

"No," Cécile tells herself, "I don't want it, I don't want anything of this icy night here, this cold, this sadness, this death.

I don't want it—" She rushes out of the salon, and through the dark corridor she reaches her parents' room, she pulls open the closet, her hands feel their way among the fabrics hanging there. . . .

Next to the bed, she remembers, there is a candle. Cécile finds some matches that Maurice gave her the other night, real matches that light—American matches. What a luxury—matches that light instantly when you scratch them on the box.

In the light of the candle, Cécile inspects her mother's gowns, dresses from before the war, and here is one that her mother wore in those days, a red satin dress, low-cut, magnificent. Cécile smiles, for she feels her pain leaving her, she smiles the way an invalid does as the grip of pain is broken by an injection.

Hastily, she rips off her dress, throwing it to the floor as she pulls her mother's ballgown over her head. The silk glides down on her bare shoulders, caresses her bust, her hips, her flanks. Cécile turns toward the mirror. At first she sees nothing but the candle trembling in the glass, like a flame reflected in a lake, then she divines rather than sees her own form, so small, so lost in this long gown that comes down covering her feet, and with her braid down her back, and her thin virgin's arms.

"Like this," she tells herself under her breath. She undoes the braid, and lifts up the golden mass of her hair, part of which falls over her face. She sticks in a few hairpins and combs, and then hunts in the armoire for high-heeled slippers, also dating from before the war.

It's Christmas, she's going to stay up for the *réveillon*, and it's absolutely necessary that she should be beautiful and that Maurice should tell her that she is pretty, Paris is liberated, and the war will soon be over and her parents will come back.

For eight days she has been oscillating between this constant state of remorse, remorse at being sad, remorse at being gay, and the conviction that she is at the threshold of her life, she has been opening her eyes so as to see everything, ready to taste everything, her heart beating with curiosity and with joy of life, only to fall back again into self-disgust because there is a war and it seems to her that she has no right to have escaped it for four years, nor to taste this life as long as the war is not yet finished. In the mirror, Cécile gazes at this creature in the red dress that emerges from the shadows, a candle in her hand, and prepares to go out into the noise and the lights, while she should really be dressed in black and remain hidden in this deserted apartment. If Myette were here to talk to her . . . If Mademoiselle could take her hand and smile to her . . . It was so simple to remain still a child, life was so simple with Myette—and happy . . . Cécile presses her cheek against the mirror and closes her eyes. The filmy mirror is as cold on her cheek as the water of the river when she went swimming with Anette. Anette is going to be married soon, surely. Louise and Vincente too. Their lives are marked out in advance. They are the same age as Cécile, and all of them have spent four years together, laughing, playing tricks, whispering secrets, dreaming. Why then is she different? She alone? Because everything had been different for her. She did not belong—neither to Myette, nor to her friends, she had been "adopted," she had come from outside, she came from another life, the life of a little Parisienne. But in Paris too, in the old days—she remembered the little girl she had been, gravely silent, the only child of elderly parents, with a father suffering from an injury from the previous war. There too she had been different, detached from the life of other girls of eight, of twelve.

Only when she was with her parents—they three had formed a whole, a whole that had never been separated. There was too much warmth between them. Cécile, like a tenderly guarded plant, Cécile like a bird in a nest, with too much attention upon her, her opinion too much asked, too much obeyed—had she perhaps been nothing more than a spoiled child?

She opens the door of the library where her father sits before a blank sheet of paper lying on his desk. He smiles as he sees her standing on the threshold of the room, his mouth smiles, and his gaze is far off, there are sails and rafts and lifeboats in his eyes. . . . "Cécile," he murmurs, "I'm going to recite something to you." He recites. Cécile recalls a number of phrases—how did they go, then?

O longs ennuis des jours semblables,
Ennuis, brouillards, des jours sans histoire—

There was another phrase, come from somewhere, that had remained fixed in her memory: ". . . *les cheveux mouillés collant aux visage, avec une cape qui vole sur les épaules, comme une main qui s'agite pour dire adieu . . .*"

What was he writing, then? Poetry? A novel?

At twelve, she found such lines too romantic in tone. She had told him this, making a *moue*. "It's so romantic, Papa, you are too sentimental, too nineteenth-century!" She was already reading modern realistic novels and was constantly ashamed of anything that might be taken for exaggerated emotion. Had she wounded him? Did he hold her childish opinion so high? She recalls his beautiful hand with its long fingers, a hand that had the look of a harp—his hand poised on the white sheet before him, protecting the still unborn work.

"Yes, yes," he would say, "you are right. Come, give your papa a kiss."

How she loved him. He was everything for her, warmth, sun, beauty, goodness . . . She loved him with a total passion, and when at thirteen she had lost him, lost both her parents, she had fortunately found the warm and ample breast of Myette, upon which she might lean her childish head. It seems to her that the difference between herself and other children has been a plethora of love. She has always received love in overabundance, she has always been the only one, both at home with her parents and with Myette. Even with Mademoiselle, who for four years had always repeated to her when they were alone, "My little Cécile, luckily we have each other, the two of us, you are altogether different from the other pupils, my own Cécile."

For the first time, as she approaches her eighteenth birthday, Cécile is alone, all alone, the war has finally caught her. The war is not only a battlefield, it is a total revolution of life, a tearing out of all the roots, a destruction of all that grows, breathes, palpitates. "The war has caught up with me, the war has caught me," and Cécile looks at herself in the mirror because what she sees is no longer herself, it is the second Cécile who ran with Anette in the woodpath pierced by whirling suns, it is the second Cécile who listens and who recalls and who is always there to say, "Do you remember?" and to scrutinize every pain as well as every joy, even while the first Cécile is ashamed, and tells her, "Go away, you shouldn't be here at such a moment, peeking, curious, indiscreet, go away—"

A knocking at the door arouses her.

For once Maurice is by himself. He is wearing his fur-collared coat, and he has the look of a gold prospector, an adventurer, an explorer, or a Russian count. His voice thunders, an animal warmth emanates from his entire, vigorous body. Just short of appearing fat, he is like a thick oak or a bull.

Cécile, who for four years has lived only with women, tells herself, "He is a father, a real father who is afraid of nothing, who can protect you from everything, from the war, from cold, and from childishness." Why, then, is she still afraid of him? For the last week, he has come everyday to see her, he has given her money to live on, he has sent her flowers as though she were already a woman, he has said marvelous things to her.

"What eyes you have, Cécile, what amazing eyes! Little cat, little tigress, come tell me your stories. What a mimic you are! How comical! I feel so good with you! Do you know, I was supposed to go to a cocktail party at Gallimard's, Sartre and Genet and all our idols will be there, and I preferred to come for you—let's go out, we'll have lunch with some friends of mine, I want them to meet you."

To amuse Maurice, Cécile imitates Mlle Angelique, she repeats Discourse on the Morals of the Reverend Mére Clemence, she describes Mlle Mazoyllet and Anette. Maurice listens enthralled, never tired of Cécile's tales; he parades her among his friends, eccentrics or celebrities alike, with the pride of a collector who has found a rare object of art.

"Jean Cocteau, have you met Cécile, the daughter of my friends the Royers? Just look at that skin, that color, that hair! Have you even seen hair like that in our times? And you should hear her tell stories and mimic people! She's extraordinary, this child!"

The "extraordinary chills" delighted, lets her imagination run free. The Reverend Mére Clemence becomes more and more of a puritan, Mlle Mazoyllet is more and more beautiful, Vincente and Louise outdo each other with their quaintness, Anette goes beyond herself in her debauchery with Antoine, for Cécile must describe everything in a way that will amuse Maurice and his friends, she must not disappoint his appetite!

And yet she is afraid of him; he studies her in the candlelight, in her red dress, with her coiffure that mounts and then tumbles again in cascades.

Even Maurice, who talks incessantly, is suddenly wordless.

Doesn't he like this gown? Is she ridiculous? Should she not have dressed up like this?

But something passes in his eyes, and Cécile knows that the gown pleases him. What passes in his eyes causes Cécile to bite her lips with her white teeth, while her heartbeat quickens. She would like to erase that look in Maurice's eyes, that look that colors her own face and throat the same red as her dress. That look should not be permitted. He doesn't have the right—he is her father, she has come to him because he is the one who must help her find her parents, for he is the friend of her parents, and he is here because she is only a child who cannot live in Paris by herself.

"Child, child," it is what her father called her, the name Myette had for her, the name given her by Mère Stanislas, Mademoiselle, and Maurice himself. She can play at being a woman, of course, play at dressing up as a woman, but it is only a childish game.

Then he mustn't look at her like that!

He has brought a long package out of his overcoat, breaking the silence with a gesture of his hand. He offers her the box without saying anything, and Cécile feels herself saved. A Christmas present. Then all is well, he has re-established the order of things, he has brought Santa Claus between them, and the chimney.

Already laughing, she tears open the silken paper and opens the box.

"Oh," she says. And again, "Oh."

She is sitting down on the floor beneath a Christmas tree, and she unfolds the delicate fabric that glides upon her hands. It is a nightgown, the most beautiful, the most astonishing of nightgowns, a gown for a fairy, for a ballerina, or for a harem slave. A pale apricot gown, so transparent that one might watch the dawn being born through the silk. A long, narrow gown over which a magician's hand has flung a milky way of tiny embroidered flowers, minute white flowerheads alone, springing to life upon the delicate shoulderstraps and flowing in a rivulet to the hem below. Cécile turns and turns this wonder in her hands, incapable of uttering a word, and Maurice suddenly kneels down beside her on the floor and says, "Do you like it, my darling child?"

Then she doesn't know anything anymore. "My child"—one doesn't give harem gowns to a child. She watches, as the look that has frightened her returns to Maurice's eyes. She doesn't understand anything anymore, nothing at all—she wants to cry, but she wants to laugh with joy. And she wants to understand, at last to understand what she is supposed to do, what she is supposed to be—because she knows that she still doesn't know what to be—not yet.

He leans toward her, his face is so large, his warmth too inflamed, his arms too strong, and his masculine odor—everything is in excess. It is a man. She knows nothing of men. She knows only a father, and women.

He is going to find her out. If she lets him come nearer, he will find out the horrible secret—that she doesn't know anything, that she is in truth that very child that she has been hiding away, for the last eight days.

Cécile jumps up, clutching the gown to herself, and with burst of laughter she cries, "Thank you, Maurice, thanks, thanks, it's too beautiful, it's a marvel." Has she said it well? Like a woman? Can he hear her heart clattering? "I'm all ready—let's go out, I'm so hungry!"

He helps her put on her coat, he smiles and kisses her hand, a kiss that has only a the slightest pressure, but that Cécile would never without shame admit having felt, not on her hand, but down her spine, a kiss as painful as a wound.

"Yes, hurry," he says, "we'll be late, there's a whole gang waiting for us at Mme Brodetzky's, she has prepared an absolutely sensational dinner."

"Hurry"—it's Maurice's password. What would he do without that word? He repeats it a hundred times a day. Without his "hurry," what would Cécile do? It has saved her quite a number of times already, during the week.

Below, a taxi waits, and in the taxi, on the way, Cécile embarks upon an animated story. She must keep things in motion with Maurice, she must talk so as not to allow a dangerous silence to establish itself.

"I wonder what Mademoiselle is doing now?" It's true that her thoughts always return to the two women who have been mothers for her, Myette and Mademoiselle. But Mademoiselle is too young to be her mother. Once again, Cécile describes her to Maurice. "If you knew how pretty she is, so blonde, a white blonde, almost a Nordic blonde—she must have English or Danish blood in her. Her skin smells so good, an odor of lavender, a scent of citronella—do you know what citronella is? It scarcely exists anymore, it's a perfume of 1900, and it's unfashionable now, it's got an acid scent. When we were alone, Mademoiselle would take me in her arms, and seat me on her knees—she began this habit when I was thirteen and had just come to Myette's house from Paris. I still didn't have any school friends then, I didn't know a soul, I was terribly unhappy at the start. Mademoiselle knew that my parents were in the Resistance. She was a real patriot. We used to listen together to the London radio—Maurice Schumann speaking in the name of General de Gaulle, in my school desk, I made a secret altar, with a Cross of Lorraine and a photo of the General. No one except Mademoiselle knew about it.

"At night I used to go to her room, with the excuse of reviewing my lessons, the night would fall, but we didn't light the lamp. Sitting on her knees, with my head on her breast, I felt so good, I felt myself protected, reassured—she was mine, I was hers—"

Cécile's voice becomes veiled. It is true that she loved Mademoiselle with a love that was pure and impassioned. But Maurice's voice too becomes veiled when he asks, "And then? And after that, what happened? Tell me, my darling child, tell me—"

Cécile, suddenly wide awake, stares at him and begins to laugh.

"But nothing, of course! Sometimes we would kiss each other, and then I would go home to Myette."

They were the most chaste of kisses, but something in Cécile finds amusement in keeping him ignorant.

And besides—whatever it was that was between them—could it really have been so chaste? *Les Chansons de Bilitis* that they read together . . . the warm room . . . the perfume of Mademoiselle . . . Of course, nothing had ever happened. But something might have happened . . . something . . . Cécile herself doesn't know what. She would not have been able to explain. Something staggering—some loss of herself . . . tenderness, caresses that she had never even imagined, but that she had divined though reading certain very beautiful poems of Verlaine, of Baudelaire, of Pierre Louÿs.

In the taxi, Cécile feels Maurice's stare resting heavily upon her. There, in the shadow beside her, she hears him breathing very heavily, as though he were deep in sleep, or in pain.

WHAT ARE YOU thinking of, Cécile, in the month of December, 1944? Of the war that is ending? Of the war that keeps on? Of the past? Of the future?

The days march uniformly by. In the morning, habituated to rise early, you dress, you slip a piece of gray bread into the ersatz coffee, you go out. You must find your Paris again, the streets, the odors, the various tints of the sky—and besides, what else is there to do but walk?

There are her father's papers, Cécile does not dare touch them. There are the forbidden manuscripts, imprisoned in their leather bindings. But her father alone can authorize her to read them. When he returns from the camps—then Cécile will ask his permission. As for the apartment, it is Maurice who busies himself with having it registered in Cécile's name; it is no longer to be requisitioned.

Each day, the front stretches a little further toward the German border. From one day to the next, there might come news of the Royers. "Wait a few more days," Maurice counsels her, "don't go back yet to Gascony." The worst is that Cécile has too soon become habituated to the presence of Maurice, to seeing him arrive in a jeep or taxi, always in a hurry, always surrounded by friends, always on the brink of some astonishing idea. Every evening she goes out with him, to films, art expositions, the theater—to the life of Paris, beginning again despite the blackout, despite the German parachutists.

On the Champs Élysées, there is a huge movie theater presenting American films for the armed forces; there is the dancing in the military clubs, new nightclubs are already opening up. After the silence of the countryside, it is exciting to be going out with grownups who are twice your age and who are so amusing and who are Paris celebrities.

But as for the nightgown—Cécile doesn't tell Maurice that she never wears it. She keeps it at her bedside in its box, wrapped in its silken paper, and before going to sleep she opens the box and looks at the gown, without being able to feel that she has the right to wear it.

The apartment is so big, so empty at night. Another thing that Cécile does not tell Maurice is that she is afraid of sleeping there alone. Once and for all she has established for Maurice this personality that is herself, yes, but is not all of herself—a Cécile filled with drollery, a tomboy who will dare anything at all, who fears nothing at all. At times, Maurice's gaze rests on her, and flickering in his eyes are the thoughts that upset her, but she has found the way to protect herself from such moments. She laughs, she dances, she makes fun of Maurice, she play-acts the child, she play-acts the woman. Maurice himself perhaps becomes so befuddled that he cannot tell which of the two Céciles he really has to do with.

It is the nights that are the worst, the nights when Cécile is alone, entirely alone, alone for the first time in her life. Maurice is not there to encourage her to believe in the return of her parents. Myette is far away, and far too is Mademoiselle, whose presence always fills Cécile with the close exaltation of love. Far away are her classes, with the laughter, and the odors of the convent, the reproaches of Mère Stanislas, the garden, and Myette . . . a whole frame of life for her, and an entire world in which she might meet that Cécile who is without fear—but here there is nothing but the night. A night so total that Cécile doubles herself up, beneath the covers, in the dark, empty apart-ment, alone with the changeless thoughts that turn and turn in her head every night. Strasbourg has just been liberated, and it is in that city that they were arrested—perhaps they are still in Strasbourg? Perhaps they haven't ever been deported from there? Perhaps they are hidden in the city? Suddenly Cécile is sure of it. They are not dead, they are not even in the camps. No one would have deported an invalid of the first war. Her mother would have hidden her husband—she adored him; she would have protected him. They are in Strasbourg, that's certain. They must be there and she must go to them there. They are wait-ing for her. Then—she is bursting with joy. She is so certain now! There are no more problems—she has only a few hours to wait—how is it that she had not thought of it sooner? It was because of this that she has never been able to lose her taste for life. She is not all alone in the world, she has always felt it. How changed they will find her, so grown—they won't be able to recognize her!

But she will know them. She would recognize her mother's face even after a hundred years of separation—and her father—his calm smile, his patience in spite of the wheelchair that he could never do without, his beautiful hands resting on his knees, his eyes, so dreamy—

But if she opens her eyes in the darkness—then all her joy instantly leaves her. One has only to look at this empty apartment to know that they are dead, that there is only despair, that they will never come back. She has no one, she cannot stay forever as a burden on Myette, she must look for work, she will manage all by herself.

Her throat is so tight it hurts. If she could only cry. In the night, every night, she turns from side to side in her bed, sighing, falling asleep only to sink into a nightmare from which she starts awake, trembling, in perspiration and terror.

Then she awaits the arrival of Maurice as a deliverance.

He arrives, and she already begins to laugh when she hears him ring at the door. When he is there everything seems simple; Maurice knows everything and can manage everything. Cécile lets herself be taken out, Maurice feeds her, covers her with attentions, treats her as a woman, kisses her hand, admires her hair, her dress, and his conversation is always brilliant, filled with colorful anecdotes, with Parisian pleasantries. He knows everybody, he knows with whom each actress sleeps, he can tell her every scandal, and he knows every essential book that is about to appear.

Cécile can never keep track of all the things he is working on. He reads the scripts of films, develops ideas for plays, sends *pneumatiques* and telegrams in every direction, speaks of novels, of articles—when does he manage to do all that? With Cécile he is attentive, affectionate. If he is courting her it is in the lightest of manners, in a way so discreet that Cécile is never quite sure of his intention. Besides, the idea would not come to her that Maurice, a man of Maurice's age, could become seriously interested in her. He surely has a mistress. At times Cécile imagines this mistress for herself. It must be an actress—Maurice knows so many of them. She must be famous and very beautiful and very well dressed and very sure of herself. A real woman.

Sometimes he takes Cécile with him to meet one or another of his friends. Cécile has already become acquainted with a woman painter who was the mistress of Pascin and has a strange face framed in a helmet of black hair cut completely round in the style of a monk. She has met a blond dancer of the Folie Bergère who calls herself Linette. And a woman who writes mystery stories. And another who is an aviatress—and another who, Maurice tells her with an apology, is a prostitute. "I hope it doesn't bother you to come along with me, Bertha is a girl who helped us enormously during the Resistance, I want her to write her memoirs, she has a great deal of talent—I could do something with her story—"

"But of course not, it wouldn't bother me, what an idea! On the contrary, I have never met any prostitutes, I would be interested." And it is true that it interested her, like everything that touches on that mysterious and forbidden area—sex. The adult occupation, which children are forbidden to approach, has always intrigued Cécile—always, that is, since she first heard her classmates whisper about it, for this matter of sex which seems to constitute so extraordinary a sin can also be an occupation, she knows, as there are women, prostitutes, who "sell themselves" and there are men who go to certain "houses" where they do "forbidden things." To meet a real prostitute seems to her something just as fantastic as to visit the North Pole or to fly to the moon.

That this matter of sex could ever have something to do with her own life is altogether improbable. Cécile has been prepared only for love. The one obviously has nothing to do with the other.

"You are so young, my little girl," Maurice often tells her. "If only I were twenty years younger!" At times he shakes his head in puzzlement while Cécile prattles of Mademoiselle and Anette, and he asks, "Just what do you mean to say? Sometimes you astonish me, Cécile." But then Cécile changes the subject, feeling herself suddenly embarrassed, and on unsure ground.

"Are you coming? Quick, I'm in a hurry," Maurice tells her

once more. "I have to go to Henriette Arnaud's—she's a terrific girl with an extraordinary voice and a sensational talent. She's still in the army but as soon as she's demobilized I'm going to start her off. She'll have a wild success. Come on, Cécile. Besides—it's odd—you resemble each other—you'll see."

In the hotel requisitioned by the army, on the Champs Élyseés, Cécile sees—or rather at first hears—his new sensation. Down the corridor she hears a hoarse, low voice, a voice that sounds like no other, singing some verses of Apollinaire's:

Elle avait un visage
aux couleurs de France—
des yeux bleus, des dents blanches
et des lèvres très rouges—

"Ah! ah!" Maurice cries. "She's becoming patriotic, our Henriette, since they made her a corporal." He knocks. Henriette opens the door; she is wearing a long blue dressing gown, and she hugs a little dog in her arms. But what strikes Cécile first of all is her long straight hair, undone and hanging alongside her pale cheeks, her slender throat. She has very large eyes, somber, angled upward toward her forehead, the eyes of a saddened lioness, Cécile reflects. Even when she smiles, she looks grave. Inside the room, a guitar lies on the floor, while Henriette's khaki uniform is tumbled over a chair; on the bed there is a scattering of song manuscripts, handwritten, typed, and some of them printed.

"Henriette," says Maurice, "here's Cécile." This seems to suffice as introduction. Already, Maurice is seated on the bed; he pulls off his tie—he has the air of being completely at home. But he always has the air of being at home, with every woman he meets.

"Well," he says, "have you written the songs?"

"Yes," says Henriette. "I worked on them. But I don't know—"

"Let's see."

Maurice stretches out his hand for a bundle of papers, runs

his eyes over them, drumming his fingers on the sheets, whistling, humming. "It's not bad—you have to change the title— it's old hat—this one is good—I'll cut off the beginning—the melody has to be changed—you'll have to rewrite the ending for me—"

"You think so?" asks Henriette, with her solemn air.

She comes closer to the bed and Maurice puts his arm around her waist. Cécile has gotten used to this—Maurice is familiar with the ex-mistress of Pascin, and he kisses the aviatress on her throat, and he calls the prostitute "darling," and he disappears into the bathroom with the authoress of detective stories. But it is on herself that Henriette's eyes are fixed, while Maurice distractedly caresses the singer's hips, and Cécile, uneasy, goes and presses her forehead against the window.

"Who is it?" she hears Henriette ask.

"Special," says Maurice. "Sacred. This one, you don't touch."

What did he mean by that? Or else—perhaps she hadn't understood? Cécile turns suddenly, astonished. The strange eyes of Henriette still rest on her.

"Mademoiselle," says Cécile, "is it true that I look like you? Maurice said so—but I don't see it."

Henriette comes toward her slowly; she lowers her curtain of black hair toward Cécile, and for an instant her cheek presses against Cécile's. It burns.

"Is it true, Maurice?" They have asked the same question at the same moment.

"The blonde and the brunette," he says. "yes, except for the color of your hair. Wait—Cécile—just slip on Henriette's uniform, and we'll see."

Cécile is enchanted by the idea. She adores costumes—and a real uniform is even better. After all, it's an idea—perhaps she can enlist? It's true that everybody says the war is almost finished, but all the same, as soon as she is eighteen—the idea of serving General de Gaulle! Cécile has dreamed about him for four years, hanging over the secret radio, listening to the BBC from London, with Myette weeping whenever she heard the voice of Maurice Schumann coming from England: "Today, the four hundred and fiftieth day of the Resistance of the French people . . ."

Cécile glances at her father's friend. Isn't he going to step out of the room so that she can take off her dress?

Maurice doesn't budge, doesn't even look away. Henriette is brushing her long hair, in front of the mirror. They seem to find it quite natural for Cécile to undress before them. "All right," thinks Cécile, "in that case, I'm not going to play Saint Touch-Me-Not." It is a part that has never suited her.

She steps back a bit, and resolutely pulls her dress over her head; her upswept hair falls down her back when she straightens herself.

All the same, it's a much more uncomfortable moment than when she went swimming nude with Anette. Cécile is wearing only a tiny brassiere and her white panties are too small. Luckily she is still tanned by the summer sun, and her tan covers her with an even, golden sheen. She stretches out her hand for the khaki skirt just as Maurice approaches and says, "Look at yourselves in the mirror, the two of you."

It's true—they resemble each other. But couldn't he have waited until she put on the uniform to say so?

"I'm cold," says Cécile, and she hurriedly pulls on the skirt and the shirt.

"She's too quick for you, Maurice," says Henriette, smiling.

In the taxi that takes them back a little later, Maurice suddenly says, "You have a ravishing little body, Cécile. A Tanagra—that's what you look like, a blond Tanagra. But why are you afraid of me?"

How does he know this? Cécile feels herself blushing.

"You prefer your Mademoiselle and your Anette to your old Maurice, eh?"

Cécile doesn't answer him.

"And Henriette—do you like her?"

"Yes, she's beautiful. She looks sad. I'd like to be her friend," says Cécile.

"Her friend?" repeats Maurice. "Really?"

His hand comes in search of Cécile's, and as he often does, he raises the square little hand to his mouth, and presses his lips into Cécile's palm.

Cécile's heart beats quickly. She doesn't know what to do, what to say, it's always the same when it's like this—what is one supposed to do when one is afraid and when one doesn't know why one is afraid? She looks at this man's head, bent over her hand, she looks at him without budging, without drawing back her hand, startled to find, mingled with the fear that contracts her, something else, something new, something pleasurable and painful at the same time, like a shiver going down her back, while the whole inside of her mouth seems to become dry. She is thirsty. Suddenly she is devoured with thirst.

SINCE THE MONTH of January, Maurice has seems preoccupied, and several times he speaks of Cécile's parents almost in the past tense.

"There is terrible news from the camps. Some of them have been liberated—the Germans gassed all of the older people, the sick, the children—" Is there something that he knows? He says not, but then why does he seem to have the air of preparing Cécile for the worst?

And yet during this same period, hope had revived in Cécile. She writes long letters to Myette. "I am certain that they'll come back." Each night she falls asleep telling herself, "Tomorrow there will be news." It's snowing in Paris, but Cécile doesn't even feel the cold, she has already become habituated to a Paris of both luxury and hunger, to being crushed in the crowded métro, to the curious fashions of the Liberation, with its wooden soles and its pyramidal hairdo, to the failures of electric current, the gray bread; Paris seems to her more severe and more extravagant and more beautiful than all that she had dreamed. When her parents return, how she will busy herself with them! How she will take care of them, how she will make them forget all of their suffering! How good it will be to have them. To have a father again. A father—that is what she has missed most, in these four years.

"I'll come at four o'clock," Maurice said, and once more she waits for him, ensconced in her parents' big bed, her favorite place of refuge, where she reads, writes letters, and munches on walnuts sent to her by Myette.

BUT MAURICE HAS arrived, and not alone. He is accompanied by Henriette and a large young man who has the air of a painter or a writer; his hair is too long, and he has the look of so many of the young people who surround Maurice, writing books or painting abstract pictures which Maurice encourages and criticizes in the same breath.

Cécile brings them all into the salon. They have a solemn air. Maurice coughs. Henriette looks angry. Cécile brings her walnuts, and offers them around, but no one accepts any and the silence stretches on between them. What do they want, then? Maurice looks at Henriette, and it is she who turns to Cécile.

"Cécile," she says finally, very quickly, and in a single burst, "you mustn't go on hoping, there has been news, they are dead."

SINCE THE MOMENT when the blow fell, it seems to her that she has run the whole way to Myette. She doesn't remember having cried. She went into her room and packed her valise. Maurice, Henriette, and the young man—all of them were talking, but she heard what they said only through the other Cécile, the shadow who listened and took note.

". . . She ought to cry, it would comfort her . . . Give her something to drink, Maurice . . . What are you going to do? . . . Where is she going? . . . We can't leave her . . ."

Without knowing how, she was in the train and Maurice was saying at the door, "My dear, my dear child, Myette will be waiting for you at the station—you'll write to me? I'll come to see you, as soon as I have a minute—you promise me, you'll go and see the doctor with Myette? I don't like to see you so pale, so tense." Hours and hours in the train without a thought. The train said, "All alone, all alone, never again, never again—" She would never see them again, then. But weren't they already dead for four years? Hadn't she lost them forever, four years ago?

At the station there is Myette—her arms, her warmth, the arms closing in again around Cécile. Then her house, a large bed, the bed of Myette, piled so high with a red eiderdown, and Cécile dressed in a long nightgown of Myette's, of rough linen, like the country nightgowns of long ago.

Only then, in Myette's arms, in Myette's bed, in her gown—only then had she been able to release the flood of tears, without danger of dying. For one night, one night alone, she had dared to show her weakness to Myette.

From the next morning on, it was finished. She had come to breakfast combed, dressed, serious, and dry eyed. No, Myette should not see her suffer, no one should see her suffer.

"IT WAS CRUEL to tell her like that," says Henriette. "I hate myself, but I didn't know how to do it. You gave me the dirty job because you're cowardly—cowardly like all men faced with sorrow. It was for you to tell her, but no, you keep it for yourself to speak to her of love. Death—that's for me."

Henriette rages on; she strides back and forth in the hotel room, throwing her clothes onto the floor, shaking her black mane. "I liked her, that little girl—and so you were jealous and you preferred that that particular memory should always be associated for her with me."

Maurice says nothing. He knows women too well not to know that when they are in anger, it is best to remain silent. Sitting on Henriette's bed, he lowers his head with a guilty air, an attitude that is always successful for him.

Little by little Henriette calms herself; she sits down at the table, lights a cigarette. "Have you any news of her?" she asks.

"Yes, but only through her godmother. She's getting along all right. She's young and at her age everything passes, all the sorrows . . . Her birthday is coming in a few days. She'll be eighteen—can you imagine it? She's really just a kid. Four years younger than you. That's not so great a difference, and yet you are a woman, and she is a child. An odd sort of child—I never seem to understand her, I never seem to understand what she knows, what she wants, what she does and what she doesn't do."

"That's what attracts you. You—Maurice Henry, the expert on women—and how he has found a would-be woman that he simply cannot understand." And she adds in English, "What a challenge!"

"Well, then, what do you advise me? What should I do now?"

Henriette begins to laugh. "But I really don't know—send her a birthday present, or go see her, or telegraph her to come back. It's really amusing to see you in such a state."

"I love her," says Maurice.

"Love—you don't know what it is. Love is for women, it's not for you men, don't talk to me of love. You wanted her, that's all. Perhaps I love her, but you, you want her."

Henriette has got up, and Maurice eyes her, reaching his hand out toward her. "No," says Henriette, "go on, get out, you disgust me."

FOR CÉCILE'S EIGHTEENTH birthday, a package arrives from Paris. Once more Cécile undoes the silk-paper wrappings, and the ribbons, to decipher her name traced in the microscopic handwriting. This time it is a luxurious flask of perfume. On the accompanying card Maurice has written, "I remember having heard you say that your dear Mademoiselle smells so good—of lavender. This isn't lavender, but this smells good, too."

Cécile smiles each time she touches a drop of the perfume—so precious, so expensive—behind her pink ears. Cécile smiles because she is eighteen, and life has taken hold again. The garden has been given back to her in all its springtime glory, and the birds and the fruit and the dawn have been given back to her. Paris has faded anew into the past—with the war. They are fighting in Germany, they are fighting in Japan, but these are the last attacks of the war. Here life is so calm. Mademoiselle recites poetry. Anette is engaged, Louise is learning stenography and typing, Vincente is in love with a boy in the army. And yet at dawn when Cécile goes down into the garden, a shawl over her shoulders and the shears in her hand, when she bends over a rose, or reaches to a branch of the walnut tree, she seems again to hear the voice calling her, "Cécile, my darling child—"

He had half-opened, in Paris, a door to another life. Cécile remembers the discussions in the cafés, and her success when she mimicked Mére Stanislas, she remembers Henriette and the other girls with their long hair and the faces of poets and painters, and the thundering voice of Maurice, "Quick, quick, Cécile, I'm in a hurry—" She remembers too the thirst that came into her, and the head bent over her palm, the taste of that red avid mouth in her palm—a drop that only makes you thirstier. "No," she tells herself, "all that is finished, it's not for me, I belong in the country here, to this countryside, to the woods, to these ramparts, to the dawns of Gascony, my place is with Myette, for always."

Once again it is dawn. Cécile is happy to have found peace again, the dawn is even more gentle, the flower petals are even more scintillating in the dew. She feels herself buoyant and whole, she marvels in astonishment at how she has been able to come to life again. But she has heard the grating of the garden gate. Cécile senses a presence in the solitude of her garden at this hour. Instantly, without turning, she feels that it is he, through the force of his presence.

And it is he, in a coat with the collar up, smiling, with his round black beard giving him the air of an adventurer. He stretches out his arms and Cécile utters a cry of joy and precipitates herself toward him.

"I've thought of you without stopping, Cécile," he says, and Cécile, with her face hidden against that large, hard chest, tells herself, "He has come for me, he has thought of me, he has missed me," and she is astonished at feeling so happy.

"Come on," says Maurice, and Cécile begins to laugh when he adds, "Quick," for even here, even in the dawn, he is in a hurry. "Come quick, I have a jeep, I'm taking you along."

"Where to?" cries Cécile, ravished. "But I'm not even dressed, Maurice," and she pulls her shawl aside to show him her long nightgown.

"And what are you doing in a nightgown at this hour in the garden, eh? Admit it, you were awaiting a lover."

Cécile wants to respond, "I was waiting for you," but she halts herself in time and only laughs.

"Then go quickly and get dressed, but the main thing is hurry up—I'm taking you to Toulouse with me, I have a meeting with the editor of a paper there."

Cécile goes to wake Myette, and dresses in a hurry. In the kitchen she finds Maurice again, with Myette serving him bread and jam and what passes for coffee since the war. They are talking politics, or rather, Maurice is talking and Myette is listening. "You'll bring her back to me tonight," she says. "Be careful, my dear—a jeep—isn't it dangerous?"

"Oh! Godmama! I'm not a baby!" Cécile cries indignantly.

What she hopes as the jeep crosses the village is that all her friends will see her in this vehicle next to this man who has the look of a real Parisian and an artist. She laughs, for she already imagines what Mlle Angelique will say behind her curtain. "Good Lord! Cécile all alone with a man—he looks like an Englishman or an actor—and in a jeep. Where is she going? She's running away, that's certain!" And she'll pull on her shawl at once and hurry to Myette.

How can she again be so happy? Is it a lack of conscience? Is it a betrayal of her parents? And yet how she loves life! How each joy, even the smallest, always fills her entirely, how she feels each joy separately with each of her sharpened senses! Like the joy now of the speeding jeep that makes her hair dance, the joy of the wind burning her cheeks, the joy of seeing the fields on both sides of the road, the fields on a morning of springtime, to breathe the odor of the earth, the odor of the trees, to hear the birds crying in the sky, to feel the sun on the back of her neck, and the warmth of Maurice's body so close to hers. This is what it means to live! To feel with one's skin, with one's eyes, with one's sense of smell, with one's hearing, and to know that all this is a gift offered her, that she has only to reach out her arms—

And it is to Maurice that she owes this morning, this happiness of feeling herself so free and young—Maurice, who is the friend of her father, who replaces him twice over, now, who has come especially for her, abandoning Paris and his friends, and his mistresses, and who has told her, "I missed you." She has been missed by this man, so amusing, so original, so filled with ideas and projects, this man whose life is a perpetual race toward more ideas and more projects, and whose presence at once transforms her peaceful and monotonous life of a little country girl into a tumult of adventures.

Maurice drives at a wild speed and the jeep bounds over the badly paved road, hurling aside a flotilla of bewildered chickens and cats.

"Well, then, my little darling," says Maurice, "tell me—I've missed your stories, too. I often think about your Mademoiselle, I imagine her with you—you'll have me meet her—and your Anette and the others too—"

Isn't he still imagining too many things that he shouldn't? Cécile is a little disquieted without really knowing why. It is true that she has exaggerated all these tales a bit, so as not to seem too provincial, too infantile for this sophisticated man. But isn't he now taking her for someone far more free than she is? It is true that Mademoiselle sometimes kissed her on the cheek, but has Cécile specified the location of the kiss for him? It seems to her that she has left this detail too vague. Does Maurice imagine for himself that because they read *Les Chansons de Bilitis*— But no, that would be absurd. Does she have the air of a masculine sort of girl?

Cécile's notions on the complexities of love and sexuality are vague and confused. With the help of her school friends, and her knowledge of country life, she has constructed for herself an understanding of things in which there is, on the one side, love, pure and romantic, and on the other side, sex, mysterious and forbidden.

Cécile says nothing and Maurice looks at her now and again from the corner of his eyes, as he drives.

"We'll make a little stop on the way," he says. "I know a wonderful inn not far from here, we can have lunch there, you can rest, we can talk a bit—"

And without knowing why, Cécile feels the same fear taking hold of her. Maurice's voice has suddenly become strange—a bit choked—and his body leans against Cécile, from time to time, with an insistence that troubles her.

As always, she detaches herself from herself, to watch. She sees Cécile laughing and pointing out the countryside to Maurice, and hears Cécile questioning him about Paris, about Henriette, and her parents' apartment, while that girl who is being watched, that other Cécile, is at the same time contracted with fear. How can there be two of her like this in a single body?

The jeep halts before an elegant inn, a real wayside inn for tourists—a sort of Trianon of Gascony. There is a thatched roof, quite new, white walls, geraniums. It is said that during the war the Germans came here with their mistresses, that there was real butter served, and white bread and ham, all through the occupation. Now, from the doorway, one hears a voice singing in English. The uniforms have changed, and another set of officers stands around the bar, perhaps with the same girls.

Here too the owner has an air of recognizing Maurice—or does he simply recognize in him the habitué of all the world's fashionable inns?

"What would you like to drink, my little darling—a glass of port? Champagne?"

"At this hour?" Cécile exclaims. "No, I'd rather have a glass of cold milk."

Maurice laughs, orders a cognac for himself and milk for Cécile.

And while she slowly drinks her milk, she feels Maurice's eyes scrutinizing her. "Cécile, come back to Paris with me," he says suddenly.

"Myette wouldn't want it," says Cécile, "and besides, what would I do in Paris, Maurice? I have to finish my school year, it's the last."

"You can live in Paris with me, in my place," says Maurice. "You needn't be afraid—why are you blushing?" But it is he who has blushed. "Cécile, since you left I've been thinking of you without a stop, incessantly. You are so young. I could be your father and still I don't love you like a daughter. Do you know that? Do you sense it? Cécile, let's go upstairs, I've reserved a room, I won't do anything to hurt you, I simply want to be alone with you. You are made for love, Cécile, with your youth, your laughter, your enthusiasm. Let me teach you—it will be better than with Mademoiselle—you'll see—"

Cécile has said nothing. Her face is afire. Her heart thumps, her knees tremble. What frightens her is not so much the words of Maurice but his face, this masculine desire on his face, in his eyes, on his lips—this desire that she has never yet encountered so totally, so brutally naked. This cannot be love, it can only be that other thing, the mysterious and forbidden thing, and Cécile feels herself falling back as from a dark pit whose bottom she cannot see.

There is but one thing to do and that is to flee. What is there that she can say, in answer to Maurice? She feels herself ridiculous, inexperienced, she wants to cry, when instead she ought to know what one should say and how one should behave in such a situation. Henriette certainly would have known, or Linette from the Folies Bergère, or any other of Maurice's woman friends.

She gets up, then, and runs out of the room—but where should she go? She hasn't any money, she doesn't know how to drive—

"Cécile," Maurice cries behind her. "Look—my darling little girl—have I offended you? But after all, you're not a little white goose—you've got too much intelligence for all that, you certainly know that this trip to Toulouse—it was only an excuse to see you, to be alone with you. It's months now that I've wanted you, that you've been driving me crazy, you know it well enough, but after all, I'm not a brute, surely you don't believe I'm going to rape you! Look at me, Cécile, lift your head, look at your old Maurice!" He is all at once so nice, his voice is no longer frightening at all, he has regained the reassuring voice of a grownup talking to a child. Cécile raises her head and sees that even Maurice's eyes, the black, glistening eyes, are no longer frightening, but smiling. She smiles, too, and lets him take her hand. "Then you're coming with me, upstairs? No, don't escape again—look, what are you afraid of, tell me? You were alone with me a thousand times in Paris, in your apartment, what difference is there? Did I ever try to violate you? Don't act like a child, it's ridiculous at your age, Cécile, we're friends. I only want to be alone with you, we'll spend a nice day together chattering, we'll have a wonderful meal brought up to the room, you'll tell me stories, we'll make plans—what's wrong with it?"

"No," says Cécile, "no."

"All right," says Maurice, "you see, I don't insist. I thought you were less provincial, that's all, more courageous, too, more of a woman. Let's go on to Toulouse."

Is he angry? Has she offended him? Has she behaved badly? A woman would surely not have refused to go up to the room with him, it's true that after all Maurice would not have forced her into anything. She must have seemed awfully stupid. In silence, Cécile follows Maurice toward the jeep. How can she get him to forgive her? How can she show him that she is so fond of him, that she has missed him, too, that above all she doesn't want to offend him? They drive along in silence now in the jeep, and all of Cécile's joy has vanished.

Can Maurice then, like a magician, bring her joy and also remove it? No one until now has had this power over her. Cécile feels herself empty and alone and abandoned; she places her hand on the seat between Maurice and herself—in that space so vacant, so large and empty, when just a little while ago there was no space at all between their two bodies.

THE ASTONISHING THING is that on the way back Maurice again becomes gay and even seems to want her forgiveness. He no longer appears angry. He chatters on about Paris. The war will be finished a month or two from now, he has come across a really sensational subject for a novel and discovered a young writer who will collaborate with him on it, he is going to begin a new gossip column in a new paper that is soon to be launched, he has a buyer for Cécile's apartment, but what should be done with the furnishings and all the papers?

"Are you already going back to Paris tonight, Maurice?" Cécile asks, disquieted. My God, how sad she will be without him.

"Do you want me to stay?" he asks at once.

"Of course," says Cécile, "you know very well that I'm glad when you're with me."

"Is that true?" Maurice stops the jeep, and takes Cécile's hand. "Then, Cécile, if it's true, at least you'll let me kiss you?"

Can she still say no and lose him again, now that she has begun once more to live?

She extends her cheek toward Maurice, but Maurice only sniffs the cheek and instantly his mouth is on Cécile's mouth, his arms encircle Cécile's shoulders, his body is pressed against hers. It is so rapid, so powerful, too, that Cécile doesn't have time to think, or even to let herself be observed by that other Cécile. She feels a slight burning on her mouth, and already Maurice has moved apart and her mouth has been abandoned and the wind that grazes her lips no longer has the same taste.

It was a scarcely deposited kiss, and yet for Cécile it is the first kiss and it seems to her that a red-hot iron has been imprinted on her lips.

"No," says Maurice, "it is better not to. You excite me too much. I'll just say some more stupidities, and you'll take flight again. Let's move on."

And all at once Cécile retrieves her delirious joy. If he has moved aside of his own will, then it means that he loves her, it is not that terrifying sex, it is pure love. He has marked her with this kiss, and then he has moved aside from her body, and therefore she can give him her soul.

It is she who then throws her arms around him, and who hides her face with happiness against his neck, so strong, so reassuring.

MAURICE HAS TAKEN a room in the village hotel; he has decided to stay a few more days, so as to work on his idea for a novel. And no sooner is Maurice installed in the hotel than it seems that the entire little town awakens from a long sleep. To begin with, at the hotel, the telephone is now busy all day long. Maurice is called from London, from Paris, from Geneva; he sends off and receives the most peculiar telegrams, upon which the postmaster, when he takes his anisette on the café terrace, delivers his comments.

One of them reads: AFTER KILLING CHANTAL DE ROUGEMONT WHAT DO I DO?

"In my opinion, she must have been a collaborator," says the postmaster to his friend the telegraph operator. Another message is even more curt: FINISHED STOP SEND TWO THOUSAND FRANCS.

As soon as Cécile comes from school, Maurice has her go to the post office with special delivery letters and packets of papers. His room is filled with newspapers, books, manuscripts that have come bursting out of his valise. The entire little town talks about him, quoting his clever remarks, which are spread by the hotelkeeper. Mme Sabathé, who operates the restaurant, discusses his clothes. The stationer has placed a dozen books in his display window, all by Maurice Henry, and Maurice has consented to autograph copies of his works.

At the table at Myette's, Maurice keeps up an endless flow of stories which Cécile is never tired of hearing. What Sartre said to Camus a week ago, and the secret life of Danielle Darrieux, and the recipe given him by the aging and famous writer Colette, who lives in an apartment in the Palais Royal, and the forthcoming books at Gallimard, and the announced return of Charles Boyer, and the next Picasso exhibition— Maurice leaps from painting to literature to fashions and to cookery, to music, and from music to politics . . .

Only Myette, when she is alone with Cécile, does not have the air of approving him. She never speaks badly of anyone, but simply keeps silent, puckering her brows and sighing.

When Cécile asks, "Isn't he amusing and intelligent, Godmother?" Myette murmurs something incomprehensible, and lets drop a plate that breaks on the stone squares of the kitchen floor.

Seated at the table, her braid over her knees, Cécile listens like a good girl, but Maurice lets his black eyes rest on her and she blushes; she thinks of the things Maurice said to her, and of the kiss, and she blushes, and she knows that Maurice knows what she is thinking, and it is a secret between them.

After dinner Maurice always says to her, "Will you walk back with me as far as the hotel, Cécile?" He has a horror of being alone even for a moment—this, Cécile has realized. She likes to walk beside him. For a man of his age and corpulence, Maurice has great agility. He walks quickly, he always has the air of an animal in excellent health, with his powerful torso, his shirt open at the throat, his silken scarf fluttering, his white teeth gleaming.

She has introduced her school friends to him, Anette with her little round face, Louise, timid and dark, Vincente with her flirting eyes. But Maurice, who at once exerted his charm for them, told Cécile as soon as he was again alone with her, "They are very nice, but they're ordinary little girls, they don't have your vitality, your spirit, your air of a doe . . ."

The one he wants to meet is Mademoiselle, and Cécile is not very eager to introduce her to him. With all the ridiculous ideas he has made for himself, she knows he will only be disappointed—disappointed in her, too, perhaps.

She has not seen Mademoiselle alone a single time since Maurice has been there, and she feels guilty, for until now Cécile has gone to see Mademoiselle almost every evening.

Maurice has gone back early to the hotel today to work, and on leaving him, Cécile decides to take a walk on the ramparts. It is only ten o'clock and there is a great pale full moon. Mademoiselle loves to walk in the moonlight; perhaps she will be there.

But as Cécile walks in the narrow little streets built during the time of the Roman occupation, the silent, empty little lanes with their houses linked from one wall to another by light arches, it seems to her that someone is following her. A step resounds now and again behind her, yet when she turns there is no one. She is somewhat frightened and walks more quickly. Here are the ramparts, and sure enough the familiar silhouette is there, seated on the great ancient stones, enveloped in a cape. Cécile makes out the blond hair looking white in the night, and at once feels her heart filled with a pure joy at seeing Mademoiselle alone again.

"Cécile! How odd it is, I was just thinking of you."

The gentle hands come to rest on her shoulders, and all at once Cécile knows for certain the identity of that shadow hiding at the entrance of the lane—it can only be Maurice. What has suddenly come over her? Is it to make him forget the way she was the other day at the inn, so terrified, with her infantile fear, is it to prove to him that she is not at all such a child, and that the things he believes of her are true, that she is more complicated, more ripe than her age, and that the tales she tells him are real?

For Cécile finds herself seized by a little demon of malice. What harm can there be in playing the game? Since Maurice after all is so fond of her tales and her fantasies, what harm is there in playing out such a story, in writing with her hands and her mouth, for him the writer, a story entitled "Cécile, or How to Impress Maurice."

Cécile puts her arms around Mademoiselle's shoulders, and places her head against her neck. "I'm cold," she murmurs.

"What's wrong, my little one? Don't you feel well? Is something troubling you?" Mademoiselle opens her cape, enfolding Cécile within it, and presses the girl to herself. From a distance they make a single shadow on the ramparts, a shadow with two blond heads pressed cheek to cheek. And in a clear voice Cécile begins to recite:

Elle entra et passionément
les yeux fermés à demi, elle unit
ses lèvres aux miennes et nos langues
se connurent—

Jamais il n'y eût dans ma vie
un basier comme celui-là—

"Oh, Cécile," murmurs Mademoiselle, "not so loud! Someone might hear you! You have no idea what you're reciting!" But her arm presses Cécile a little more strongly against herself and Cécile, forgetting the game, feels herself strangely moved.

"Excuse me for interrupting you, mesdemoiselles, will you permit me to join you? Cécile, won't you introduce me to your friend?"

Then it is all right, and he has been caught in her little game as by a trap. Cécile detaches herself from Mademoiselle. How brightly Maurice's eyes shine in the dark. Suddenly Cécile feels sad, and terribly guilty.

"I MUST GO home, it's late," she says.

"I'll walk with you," Maurice says at once.

Mademoiselle, who lives just by, in the convent, descends the huge stone steps running lightly. She turns back once and smiles; her hands are white in the shadow of the cape that opens behind her when she runs like that.

Cécile follows her with her eyes until her hand, her blond hair, her cape have all disappeared through the little doorway behind the convent. Then Cécile goes homeward with Maurice, in silence, passing along the empty lanes with their closed shutters. Maurice doesn't speak. He only takes Cécile's hand into his, and Cécile leaves him her hand.

On emerging from the narrow lanes, one may come home to Myette's through the main street, or by way of the public garden called the Bastion. It is through the deserted Bastion that Maurice takes her, this garden where Cécile, long, long ago, when she was hardly more than a baby, used to play, sitting on the ground with her little pail and shovel, scooping up the chestnuts that fell from the trees. There are benches in the garden, and Maurice, still without saying anything, sits down on one of the benches, facing a round platform encircled by a grill, the platform of the Sunday concerts. The orchestral kiosk is empty behind its wrought-iron balustrade. Cécile sits down beside Maurice. In the darkness and the silence she seems to hear an orchestra playing as in a dream, invisible behind the bandstand's ornamental grill.

She knows that Maurice is going to kiss her once again, and this time she awaits the kiss.

He has put an arm around her shoulders. It's strange that he isn't in a hurry. Maurice silent, Maurice stirring slowly—it's so extraordinary.

But he doesn't kiss her. Not yet. He speaks. He begins to tell her stories of his travels, stories of his youth, he talks of a book that he has dreamed of writing and that he hasn't yet written. And then, only afterward, he places a single finger against Cécile's cheek, and turns that cheek toward him, very gently, like a hypnotist beginning his spell. Cécile offers her mouth closed and her eyes open. She feels herself already experienced, this time. It is her second kiss. It's agreeable no longer to be afraid. Little by little her eyes close, her lips half open. The invisible orchestra has stopped playing its music, she hears no more than the jerky breathing of Maurice.

And he says, "Don't be afraid of anything, stay like this, don't move, give me your hand . . ."

He guides Cécile's hand to his own body, and despite the clothing, Cécile feels, beneath her hand, something warm and hard. It is strangely like touching a little cat, a little bird. She has no fright from this strange contact under her hand, for she has caressed so many kittens, so many starling, that her hand curves of itself in tenderness. But suddenly she looks at Maurice and her hand stops. It is Maurice's face that frightens her, it is not his unknown body.

Maurice is not there with her; he is so far away, he has departed elsewhere. His face is a mask, without eyes, without a mouth. This hard mask, this figure that is seated at her side and has taken the place of Maurice—what is it that could so have detached him from her? What is it that could have taken him away and replaced him by this mask that little by little immerses itself in some solitary enjoyment, totally solitary, an enjoyment that brings a sigh from the mask, such as she has never heard. A solitary enjoyment that spreads over this mask like a blush that suffuses a face with shame.

"Maurice!" Cécile cries, in terror.

The mask makes no reply. Then the mask seems to dissolve slowly, the face of Maurice reappears. The eyes reappear, and the mouth. Maurice has returned to her side, on the bench in the garden, and Cécile, astonished, watches this metamorphosis as Beauty must have watched the fading away of the Beast.

SHE STILL FEELS guilty the next morning when—since Myette has no telephone—a message comes from the hotel to her house.

"It's M. Henry. He asks that Mademoiselle come quickly to the hotel, as he has received a telegram and must go back to Paris."

Cécile is seated at the kitchen table, doing her Latin lessons; her braid hangs down her back, she writes with her elbows spread out on the table, biting her lower lip, and scratching one leg on the other.

"Right away?" asks Myette. "And your lessons, Cécile?"

But Cécile is already standing. He's leaving—he's going away—she can think of nothing else. In the street, she begins to run, without a thought for appearances. To get there more quickly she cuts across a field, leaping over a goat track, rejoining the main street further along. No, after this time he won't come back, he is going away forever. And the thought of living without him now seems utterly impossible, while the idea of living with him seems even more impossible.

Cécile bursts into the hotel, climbs the stairs four at a time, knocks at the door and opens it without even waiting for an answer.

It's true that he is leaving—his valise is open on the floor and Maurice is throwing into it, pell-mell, his books, manuscripts, and shirts. He stops, nevertheless, staring at Cécile, framed in the doorway, gasping from having run, her eyes circled, her mouth sad, and now he advances toward her without saying a word, he closes the door behind Cécile. He takes hold of the end of her long braid and draws her gently toward him, by her braid, like a fisherman pulling on the cord of a net in which an imprisoned fish flutters.

And Cécile lets whatever happens happen, she lets herself go completely, hypnotized, emptied of resistance, divided between fear and the desire to be done with it so that she will no longer have to defend herself, no longer have to make any decision. Isn't it so much simpler, at bottom, to let what happens happen?

Maurice's hand comes to rest upon her, in one place and another, upon her neck, her face, her knees . . . like a little animal in itself, quite separated from Maurice, a little animal that comes to touch and sniff her, that glides over her, that descends and remounts, turns about her throat where a single vein beats wildly, stops on the button that fastens Cécile's white school collar, a little "Claudine collar" that is part of the convent uniform. "No," Cécile sighs, but Maurice bends over her mouth, once more he drops only the lightest, briefest of kisses on this mouth. "Don't be afraid of anything, I won't hurt you, I won't do anything that you don't know already—like a woman—believe me—nothing except like a woman—"

She's caught in a trap then; it isn't Maurice who is caught in her trap but she herself.

"It will be better than with her, you'll see—you don't have to be afraid of me, I love you too much, it will be much better, much better still, my little lesbian, my little lover, let yourself go, let me do it, don't be afraid of anything—"

She is stretched on Maurice's bed, watching, very close over her, that bending face, the landscape of this face of a man, the creases at the corners of his lips, the sparkling lakes of his eyes, the black forest of his beard and hair. And it is true that he knows how to make her body vibrate, and his hand can be gentle and his mouth hot, it is true that it could be agreeable if she wasn't so afraid, afraid of him and afraid of losing him, and afraid of the other Cécile who has got up, who is there, who is watching her, who judges her and who will never forget a single movement, a single detail.

She realizes that she is naked only because of the colder air on her body, and she closes her eyes so as not to see Maurice's body, terrified of looking at the forbidden place. He has said that he would not hurt her and at first it was true, it was almost agreeable, but now it is frightening, it hurts, it isn't true that it is like the gentleness of Mademoiselle's hands, now it is that gasping above her and this heavy body that crushes her and the shame and the realization that perhaps everything is a lie and that life is not beautiful, not filled with flowers, with sunlight, with youthfulness, but a sort of devouring animal. She has betrayed love with this monster posing as Maurice. Never again will she be able to love, she will be enslaved by this monster forever. And already this is true, for she forgets the pain in her astonishment over the taste in her mouth, over that intoxication in her head and that she will never again be able to live without him.

She sighs, but it is no longer the same sigh, and Maurice, hearing this altogether new sighing, presses her even more closely to him, before sinking heavy upon her.

Shortly afterward, Cécile rises, she gets up as for the second act of a play in which she must be the heroine, she sits on the same bed, with her half-undone braid, and her face that is no longer the same, that will never again be the face of a little girl.

SHE HAS FLED, she has gone back running over the same path, jumping over the same stones, taking the same turns. If she could, she would have walked in her very same footprints, as though to prove for certain that nothing has changed.

She does not want to be a woman—a woman is an adult. Cécile wants to remain what she has been until now—a happy child. The adult world has an unknown face that can change into the face of a monster, and the worst of all is that this monster might be pleasing to her; just so, the Beauty ended by being in love with the Beast. She has not changed, it isn't true—but why, then, did Maurice say *vous* to her, afterward?

Cécile runs toward Myette's house; she already sees the wall that encloses the garden reassuringly in its arms. While she dressed, Maurice had talked to her. Cécile can remember nothing of what he said, except that *vous*. Had she changed so much for him, too, then?

And yet she had not wanted what had happened to happen. He has promised her that he wouldn't do anything to hurt her, that it would be "like with a woman." She had believed that in giving way she would most quickly find herself free again, that nothing serious would happen, that she would recover all her freedom again, afterward, and the solitude of her life in the country.

But what will she say now to Myette? Won't Myette see the truth at once on her new face, so new that Maurice had ceased to say *tu* to her?

Here in the garden is the great walnut tree in whose branches Cécile had passed so many hours, in the company of the heroes of her books and the heroes of her own imagination. The walnut tree will not stare at her face, the tree will not ask a single question of her. Tenderly, Cécile takes hold of the familiar trunk, stroking it; she takes hold of the low branches and lifts herself, hiding among the thick foliage.

Only here does her heart cease to thump. Here she can wait, and go over everything, and try to understand what has happened. And her skin shivers, at what she sees anew. She hears the voice of Maurice, she listens to the sighing of Cécile—and it is the other Cécile who is present, there, and who now in the walnut tree whispers to her, *remember this*, and *remember this*. And as she remembers, something else is born in her—a strange desire—is it already the monstrous poison circulating in her blood? Why does she think, blushingly, of Maurice's hands?

The garden gate grinds. Cécile bends her head between the branches. It is he; and in the half-darkness that falls over the garden at this hour, she hears his voice. "Cécile, where are you?"

He knows, then, that she has taken refuge in the garden. He knows with the instinct of a hunter. Cécile does not want to reply, and yet a voice says "Yes," and Maurice raises his head toward the walnut tree.

He comes closer. Cécile studies him through the branches,

from the top down, with the fearful and provoked air of a cat that has taken flight into a tree. Maurice catches sight of the slender, supple body in the old-fashioned convent uniform, of the long honey-colored braid and the oblique eyes observing him unblinkingly. A leg encased in a gray cotton stocking rises toward the bent body, the wide-pleated skirt is spread over the branches.

"Cécile," says Maurice, "come down, I must speak to you, I've already missed my train for Paris. Cécile, we can't leave each other like this, now look!"

He is answered only by the silence and the night descending on the garden; he feels himself ridiculous and guilty, under this tree, begging this obstinate child to come down and talk to him.

"Cécile, after all, I can't climb up and join you there in the tree, can I? Do you see me climbing among the branches at my age? What will I look like!"

Cécile begins to laugh. The image that at once appears to her, of Maurice clambering among the branches of the walnut, is too comical, so comical that she instantly forgets all her pain and anger. And then, she must certainly admit to herself that she is glad that Maurice is here, that he didn't leave.

Slowly, she begins to descend. A slender leg slides toward Maurice from beneath the foam of an embroidered petticoat. How charming she is in her school uniform, with her braid, and how sweet that pliant little body was to hold in his arms, only a while ago. Maurice seizes hold of Cécile's waist when she comes down to his height, and lifts her to the ground.

"Come to Paris with me, my darling little girl, I don't want to leave you and I can't stay here forever."

"No, I can't," says Cécile, "you know perfectly well that I can't."

"And if I marry you—can you?" asks Maurice suddenly, and the words have come out even before he knew he was going to say them.

Marry him? But one doesn't marry unless one loves with real love. How can she marry, when what there is between them is this monster, only sex with the face of temptation?

Cécile is so astonished that she stares at Maurice and begins to laugh.

"I can't marry you, Maurice! Look!"

She has so convinced an air that Maurice feels offended.

"And why not?" he demands, suddenly fully determined to marry Cécile.

"Why, because, because—" Cécile doesn't know what to say. How can she explain to Maurice that one gets married in white in the village church to a very pure young man whom one loves only with love?

"I can only be your mistress now," she says at last, "because what there is between us—it's only what happened just before." She lowers her head, and Maurice doesn't understand at all. This child is astonishing him, but the desire in him returns, and more strongly than before. Because he has tasted of Cécile, he is only the more hungry for her now, and he is certain that he who has never been faithful to a woman cannot love without this one. And how envious all his friends in Paris will be of him for having a young wife of eighteen, so strangely beautiful and fresh and droll. After all, if he has to get married one day, it is just as well to marry Cécile.

"Cécile, I'm going straight to your godmother to ask permission to marry you, you're not going to refuse?" He placed his hand on Cécile's throat. This animal hand that Cécile recognizes at once—this time it brings a shiver through her entire body. There is it, she is enslaved to this hand, she knows it, she has been enslaved, she has tasted the poison, and she cannot do without it.

"Oh!" cries Maurice. The sudden physical reaction of Cécile seizes and upsets him, too. This hand of his—has it really acquired such a power over the body of another being? Desire swells through his body to the point of pain. He wants Cécile instantly and for always.

And the door of the house opens. Myette appears, lighted from behind as in some Flemish painting. Her worried voice calls, "Cécile, is it you in the garden?"

"Yes, Godmother," cries Cécile, "I'm coming." Maurice follows her, and in the shadows, he takes her hand.

ON THIS NIGHT the electric current in Myette's house is cut again, as so often in the beginning of 1945. Cécile undresses in the light of a candle. Naked in her cold room, Cécile shivers and reaches out her hand for her pajamas, when suddenly she has a change of idea. She goes to the armoire, the ancient armoire whose wood has been polished by the years, she opens it, and from beneath a pile of linen she takes out a packet wrapped in silken paper.

Now she may. Now she has the right for the first time to wear this nightgown meant for a woman. The transparent gown slides from her shoulders to her ankles, and clings to her body with a living pliancy.

Slowly, Cécile advances toward the mirror; she studies herself for a long while. Is this really she? In truth, isn't this really she? With one hand she lifts her heavy braid, rolling it at the top of her head.

"Mme Maurice Henry," she says to the young woman in the mirror. "How are you, Mme Maurice Henry? Have you been living in Paris long? No? You are only just married? To the famous Maurice Henry himself! What an exciting life you must lead, madame, how I envy you!"

THE NEXT MORNING Maurice has gone back to Paris, leaving behind with Myette a little fiancée who no longer knows whether she should rejoice or weep. But Myette, for certain, does not rejoice. All the refugees have gone from the village, returning to their homes; Myette has no more Spaniards, or Jews, or Communists, or Gaullists to shelter, to nourish, and now Cécile too will leave—and leave with a strange man who creates too much noise around himself, whose profession is rather difficult to define, who is twenty years older than she and who has a doubtful moral reputation. But what can be done? Cécile has declared that she wants to become a woman, and he has declared that he wants to marry her.

Myette does not feel she has the right to interfere. Cécile is eighteen, she must make her own life decisions, and besides, isn't it better for her to go to Paris and to live there in the world of artists and intellectuals than to remain in this sleepy little village perhaps only to inherit a life as solitary as that of Myette herself? Cécile has too many gifts, Myette knows. Her eyes are too lively, they see everything, they note everything. She could become so many things, in Paris. Isn't she the best actress in her school theater? All the parents, all the teachers, at every festival, are ceaseless in their admiration of her grace, her expressiveness, her natural way, in her mimicry, her dancing. She is also the best pupil in French composition, and this is hardly astonishing, as she had a father who wrote novels. Novels that have not been published, but all the same, entire novels, and her mother too spent her youth among painters and musicians, and was gifted, like Cécile. Cécile is so full of life and of ideas. No, it would be a crime to stand in the way of this marriage. It is necessary that she leave, that she begin her own real life. Myette says nothing, sighs a great deal, and feeds Cécile as though she would never again in her whole life have anything to eat.

At dawn she sends Cécile into the garden to hunt for the most excellent frogs, good and green, for Cécile is delirious over fried frogs' legs scented in garlic. Every day, there are succulent omelets *aux fines herbes*, with salads from the garden, there are snails cooked by Myette as no one else how to cook them, she prepares homemade paté and boudin with applesauce, a crusty blood sausage the color of burgundy wine. "Good Lord, Godmama!" cries Cécile, her mouth full, "you'll make me so fat that Maurice won't want to marry me anymore—that's what you're plotting, I'm sure!"

But Cécile has never been able to resist a good, copious meal. She loves to eat, as she loves to swim, to warm herself in the sun, to pick flowers, to play with Myette's cats. So much energy, so much joy of life—if only that man, that stranger from Paris, will not use it in vain, if only he will not spoil this young girl, so fresh, so happy with life, that Myette is letting him take away, against the counsel of her own heart.

Already, since her engagement, Cécile has changed. Maurice went off the next morning, but Myette senses that Cécile is no longer the Cécile of yesterday. There is something imperceptible in her—a shadow in her multicolored eyes, a crease at the corner of her delicate lips, a different stance suddenly taken by that pliant, catlike body. "He's already changed her for me," think Myette, resentfully.

Maurice is to come back in a month for the marriage, and these weeks pass slowly for Cécile. She no longer has any desire to gossip with Anette, she no longer wants to go walking with Mademoiselle. If Mademoiselle lets a hand fall on her shoulder, Cécile now finds herself uneasy, and she draws away.

At night, each night, just as she has done for the last four year, Myette brushes Cécile's long hair before the girl goes to bed. Seated in her pajamas, Cécile closes her eyes and gives herself to Myette's ministrations, completely letting herself go. Sometimes Myette tells stories of her own childhood, in the time of gas lamps and diligences. At that period, Myette lived for several years in Paris. She had known Sarah Bernhardt and Pierre Louÿs, Apollinaire and the beautiful Otero. A whole epoch passes by in her tales, and epoch of courtesans, of painters and poets whom Cécile watches passing by for the last time under her closed eyelids.

THEY HAVE RECEIVED the blessings of the village mayor and of the church, and Maurice clutches in his own hand the square little hand of Cécile, still stained with wild berry juice, still bearing the scratches of country roots, the little hand that at last legally belongs to him—the hand, and the arm gloved in white silk, and the whole light body in the long wedding dress.

And Cécile has forgotten her fears, in the joy of seeing Maurice again after these four weeks of separation. It's true then that she is his wife and she is leaving at once with him for Paris.

She is the wife of a famous author, of a literary critic, a journalist, a film producer—for Maurice is so many things at one and the same time! A hero of yesterday, a celebrity of today—it's strange, nevertheless, to be his wife or the wife of any man, since until now she has not belonged to anyone. In the midst of the reception Maurice comes whispering to Cécile, "Quick, my darling little girl, the car is waiting, let's leave without anyone seeing us."

And Cécile has time only to catch her cat, who is leaving with them. She laughs like a schoolgirl escaping from class, while she follows Maurice down the corridor and they flee through the kitchen door, with Minou clutched in her arms.

AND THE FIRST night, in a hotel on the road to Paris, Cécile tells herself that now everything will be different. Now they are married, and so her love-making will be with love, it will not be that other thing. She is his wife, and besides, she knows everything now, she is no longer afraid.

She repeats this to herself while she undresses with trembling hands.

PART 2

Cécile opens her eyes. She is still unable to habituate herself to waking late, in Paris. At dawn she opens her eyes wide all at once, ready to leap from her bed, to run into the garden, and then, suddenly, she remembers. She doesn't need to turn her head to know that her husband is there, sleeping at her side. Lying on her back, motionless, she studies the dismal room around her with the same desperate look that this dwelling evoked in her from the first day.

She had got out of the car with Maurice, the driver behind them, dragging the trunk filled with her trousseau, packed and prepared by Myette; Cécile still clutched to her breast a terrified Minou. It was here, then—the street where Maurice lived?

Once more she read the name on the sign, RUE VISCONTI, a narrow street, so dark, so sad, without trees.

"Come," said Maurice, taking her hand. She followed him, mounted a stairway, entering the apartment behind him.

Was this where he lived, then? Where she would live? A row of rooms, all dark and horribly furnished, with disorder everywhere, as though some thieves has just fled. Behind the dirty windows, with their gray grimy curtains, a high brick wall offered the only view, and in the rooms, piles of yellowing newspapers were dumped on every piece of furniture and scattered over the bed.

Approaching the half-opened bureau drawers, Cécile had found them overflowing with photographs and postcards. The first picture she had picked up had brought a cry of astonishment from her, and Maurice had hurried to her laughing, taking the photo from her hands. "Of course, you had to tumble on a dirty picture right away! Ah, these children! They always go straight where they shouldn't! I have a whole collection of pornography but it's not for right away, not yet, you're too young. I'll show them to you—next week!" He laughed at his joke, and Cécile set down Minou and began to laugh, too. After all, she was not going to let herself be discouraged by a dark apartment, by a photo of the sort that every soldier, it seemed, carried around. Maurice was a man, and all the men had been soldiers, these were souvenirs of the army, these shocking photographs—it was nothing. Above all she didn't want to give Maurice the impression that he had married a little provincial. Besides, the best thing was to get used to everything, at once. And so Cécile went back to the drawer, opened it, and took out the photo. It was really ugly, the men wore only his socks and the two women were heavy, badly made up, and they looked nasty. An involuntary grimace crossed Cécile's face, like when she had to swallow castor oil as a little girl. Watching her out of the corner of his eye, Maurice smiled "So you like it already?" he asked.

She remembers this, as she lies at his side while he sleeps.

A church bell sounds the hour, and a heavy gust of wind

seems to blow past the windows. It is the beating of the wings of a flock of pigeons, taking flight. Maurice's hand comes searching for the tail of her braid, pulling Cécile closer to him, and Cécile bends, consenting, and astonished—her astonishment never ending. Just as at the dawn, in the past, she had bent down to her garden, to her plants, her animals, seeking to understand and to know, in the same way now her curiosity, as avid as always, bends her toward the strange movements this man has for her. What will he invent anew? What more will he show her?

Already, she has understood so many things that the Bible and her catechism let her hear about, without explanation. These "sins of the flesh," these "infamous practices," these "unnatural acts"—all these things are offered to her every night, ever morning, by Maurice in the legality of their marriage. It is really incredible. With docility, Cécile learns, like a diligent student—above all never daring to show her surprise or even her aversion, always too much afraid to be taken for a child or a little provincial.

In any case, Maurice has very little time to devote to her. From the moment he is up in the morning he is in a hurry. As they have not yet found a maid, they go down to breakfast at the zinc counter of the corner bistro. The proprietor salutes them every morning as acquaintances, "Everything going all right, M. Henry? And the little lady—everything going all right?"

After having hurriedly dunked a croissant in his café au lait, while he reads his morning paper, Maurice is ready to launch himself into Paris. Cécile gulps the tepid and tasteless café au lait while thinking of the steaming café au lait perfumed with chicory that she was so used to consuming, with her healthy appetite, in the convent school only a few weeks ago.

"Quick," says Maurice. "I'm late." He deposits a kiss—already conjugal—on the forehead or cheek offered him by Cécile, he stops a taxi and disappears. Where does he go off to, like that, every morning? To the paper, Maurice says, to the printer, so that little fellow who promised to do an article for him, or to speed up that American who is supposed to do a sensational story about the German women who prostitute themselves for a pack of cigarettes, to the Swiss who wants to put money into a film, a sensational idea of Maurice's, for which he has to find someone to write the scenario, and then he has to drop in at a painter's, and he has to do something about getting that actress started again—he can't manage to get everything done by himself . . . He runs from morning to night, sending off his telegrams, his *pneumatiques*. The telephone rings all day long in the apartment; "M. Henry?" ask the voices of men, of women, with English, Polish, Russian, American accents, and always the message is "It's urgent."

Cécile take refuge in her room, on the bed. She has always loved to read and dream. Perched on a bed in place of a tree—there is no tree to climb in Paris, so her life has installed itself on this bed where she nibbles on walnuts, bites into an apple, sucks at a bonbon—she doesn't want to cook a meal just for herself, nor to go out into Paris. She is afraid Maurice might come home suddenly, needing her for something, and not find her.

Maurice has made some sort of arrangement for her parents' apartment, and he has brought over all the books and papers in a number of wooden crates, storing them in an empty room in the flat. "You ought to look into all that," he says, "you ought finally to read those novels your father wrote, maybe they could be published."

Cécile hesitates. The days pass—she is hesitant of opening the manuscripts that had always been forbidden to everyone, and she puts off the task from day to day.

In the evening, when Maurice returns at last, it is only to cry out, "Quick, Cécile, get dressed, we're going out." And Cécile, delighted that her solitude is ended, rushes for her coat, her gloves, pins up her hair, smiling to herself in the mirror. Yes, she had more and more the air of the real Parisienne.

AT BOTTOM, what Maurice is is a sort of factory manager, but in his factory the workers put together words. It's a veritable industry. Little by little Cécile begins to understand that her husband signs his name to everything but writes nothing. The articles, the scenarios, the criticisms, the essays, the novels, stories—all this vast production signed with the name of Maurice Henry is furnished for him by an array of impoverished and unknown young men who hang around the cafés of St. Germain-des-Prés. The genius of Maurice lies in his ability to give them ideas, to fire them with his inspiration, and he moves like a bee from one to the other, extracting here and there a new situation, another chapter, a final scene, the review of a new book, a criticism of the latest art exhibition, he drags all this booty home, classifies it, annotates it, changes it, passes it on the next day to another hand for further enrichment, and finally he produces the books and articles and films signed by Maurice Henry.

His workers are paid—they telephone to ask for the lean or the "royalties" that Maurice promised them, as the case might be. Maurice, who many not knows how to write other things, at least knows how to write checks, and he sends these off with laconic comments, "Bravo, last thing fine," or "A little short—your story—old boy—had to spend the night rewriting," or "Not bad, has to be developed."

Several times now, Cécile, on the point of opening her father's papers and straightening them out, hesitates and falls back, telling herself, "No, I can't give over my father's works of art to that commercial factory. What my father wrote was pure art, for art's sake alone. To give his books to Maurice would be to prostitute them."

And so she goes back to the big bed, curls up, hugs Minou to herself, and begins to write her long letters to Myette.

For Myette, Cécile rearranges her life in a somewhat different fashion. To please Myette and still her worries, Cécile describes her days on the Camps Elysées and at St. Germain-des-Prés, in the museums, and her evening at the gala premières, at the openings of art exhibitions. It's true, after all, that she goes with Maurice to the theater, but more often she tags along to the printing plant of a newspaper where, at one in the morning, she waits in a smoke-filled room while he bends over his pages, scratching things out, correcting, or having them rewritten by some timid young man with black-rimmed fingernails.

Afterward Maurice, who never seems to need sleep, drags her from café to café, to the Deux Magots, to the Flore, to the Rhumerie Martiniquaise, from table to table among the young creatures with long hair and dirty fingers who have ideas to sell for a few cigarettes or a glass of beer.

Henriette, the young corporal of 1944, is a civilian again and Cécile is pleased, one night to rediscover her. She is singing now in a basement café in St. Germain-des-Prés, to which Maurice drags Cécile at two in the morning.

Once again Cécile discovers that young boyish figure, the long black hair, the slanted eyes, the raucous voice—the portrait of herself, as on a photo negative—her own portrait in black, and in sorrow—a Cécile in reverse.

Henriette seems to her so much more ripe, so much more developed than herself. She feels inferior, a little fool who knows nothing of life, before this singer who talks down to men from her high perch, and who, when they are together, tells Cécile stories that shock her, though she dare not show it.

At twenty-two or twenty-three, Henriette has already exhausted a long list of lovers, men and women. She doesn't hide from the astonished Cécile that she loves women as much as men, even more. Cécile asks herself whether Maurice too has been on Henriette's list, but when she questions Maurice, he only begins to laugh. "Of course not, darling. Would you be jealous? I with Henriette? Never in my life!"

"I'm not jealous," Cécile defends herself at once. What a horror, for Maurice to think her jealous. One no longer has the right to jealousy in the twentieth century. In Gascony, perhaps, but certainly not in Paris.

"You know perfectly well that you are free, Maurice. I asked only out of curiosity, that's all."

"Cécile, hand me my lipstick," says Henriette. Cécile is spending the afternoon at Henriette's, sitting on the floor, her legs crossed Turkish style.

How beautiful Henriette is; she has a way of being wild,

and violent, that pleases Cécile. There is nothing comforting about her, as there is in Mademoiselle, but nevertheless there is something just as attractive—because she is so free. She is that which Cécile would like to be—a woman totally liberated, who is afraid of nothing and who seems already to have tasted everything. "I can never be like that," thinks Cécile, discouraged.

"LAST NIGHT AFTER I was through singing I went out," related Henriette. "I was with some friends, and there was an adorable boy, young, blond, timid—can you imagine, he was a virgin! A virgin at twenty-four!" Henriette's hoarse voice becomes tender. She examines her face in the mirror, tracing the contours of her lips with a black crayon. "He was a virgin, but he isn't anymore." She looks at Cécile. "He came with me, when I was through at the nightclub, and we went dancing. You can't imagine how wonderful it is—the body of a young man who has never yet touched a woman, a body so hard, so young, and so frightened! He explored me with such an air of wonder!"

"You can't imagine . . ." No, Cécile can't imagine it. She knows only the body of Maurice, a man of forty, and Maurice can no longer find wonder in what has to do with love; he can find excitement, but he cannot find wonder.

"He was so pure, that boy," continues Henriette, "he didn't know a thing, nothing, I had to show him everything."

For me it's the opposite, thinks Cécile. It's I who still don't know anything. And it's Maurice who has to teach me, and what he teaches me hasn't any purity at all, it cannot be pure— and I must incessantly prove to him that I'm not ashamed, that I'm not afraid, and also that he is the freest man in all of Paris. How marvelous it would be, nevertheless, to be able to love Maurice with real love, and to ask the same love of him. An absolute love, a pure and impassioned love filled with wonderment—and not have to play any sort of role for him—to love him like a father and a lover and a brother and a friend, all at the same time, and to tell him, "I'm afraid" without shame and to tell him, "I don't know a thing" without blushing and to tell him, "No, that I don't want" without compunction.

But that's impossible. Maurice would cease to love her, cease to desire her—which would be even worse, for Maurice is as indispensible to her as a drug.

HER LIFE HAS in a way then established itself, a life very different from what she had imagined. It is above all a solitary life. Maurice is almost never there during the day. Cécile, accustomed to sunlight, to long walks in the country, to the spicy and abundant provender of Myette, passes her days on her bed, as on a raft, dreaming, and feeding herself with whatever falls to her hand, fruits, and candies, like someone imprisoned in a harem. Only the telephone interrupts her reveries.

In the evening, Maurice returns, instantly filling the apartment with movement and noise, dragging Cécile into a Paris she sees only at night. And all of Maurice's friends, too, seem to be creatures of the night in this postwar Paris—his friends, his "contacts," his "assistants," his "secretaries," an entire army that works for him without a pause. Sitting in the smoke like a Buddha in a cloud of incense, a cigar in his mouth, his hands in his pockets, Maurice relates his latest projects to his entourage, his little crowd gazing on him with admiration and envy. His projects are always at the point of being realized. Charles Boyer is coming back from America especially to appear in a film that Rossellini, the Italian sensation discovered since the war, will shoot in Berlin. Marlene Dietrich has accepted a part in a play that he is writing "in collaboration." Sartre is going to write for an avant-garde magazine which he is going to start in a few weeks.

At the beginning, Cécile would become enthralled, would exclaim, but little by little she sees that few of these projects come into being, and still, Maurice continues always to be absent, and his papers pile up on his desk, the telephone never stops ringing, and the articles, the books signed with his name become so numerous that one asks oneself what room there can be for anyone else to publish anything in Paris.

What is missing to her, more and more, is a friend. Maurice is a lover, but not a friend. He listens to her only in public.

When she recounts her stories to his friends, in a café at night, Maurice laughs and becomes inflated. "Isn't she comical—my little one! Listen to her imitate the Gascony accent! . . . Tell them your story about the stationery shop in your village, and the schoolmaster, Cécile . . . and your story about Mére Stanislas and the lesson in correct behavior."

Cécile relates and mimics—it amuses him and, besides, she at last has Maurice's attention. To please him, to have him admire her, she would do no matter what.

"It's pretty, your long hair," says Maurice one morning, "but really it's out of fashion—a braid is all right for an old maid. You would look much more interesting with short hair."

Cécile doesn't even stop to think. She jumps from the bed, naked, with her hair falling loose as far as her thighs, she runs to the mirror, takes the scissors—the blade is cold against the back of her neck—and her locks sigh as though it hurts to them to be cut. Maurice, sitting on the bed, calls encouragement to her. "Well! There! It must be admitted you make a quick decision! Be careful—don't cut crosswise—I should have taken you to Carita, to have it properly done!"

But he is nevertheless satisfied with the result. "Now you look completely like Henriette."

Cécile leans her triangular little face toward the mirror—her hair now falls alongside her throat and stops in a fan on her shoulders, she feels an odd little chill passing against the back of her neck; shaking her head like a foal, she laughs, "It tickles my neck, Maurice."

As a reward, Maurice takes her that very evening to hear Henriette in a new existentialist cellar. After her turn of song, Henriette comes to sit with them; she is wearing tight clinging trousers and a black pullover with a rolled collar. She gazes at Cécile, and she smiles with that smile that always looks as if it is about to transform itself into tears. "You've cut your hair! Cécile, what a crime, such beautiful hair! I'll bet it's Maurice who wanted it!" She puts her arms around Cécile's shoulders. "What do you do all alone by yourself all day, Cécile? Don't you get bored?"

"No, I read, I think, I write to Myette." Cécile would never admit that she is alone and sad.

"What a program!" says Henriette. "Reading, thinking, writing. Why don't you come more often to see me at my place? I sleep until noon, but in the afternoon you could come, we'll go out for a walk. Do you like the street fairs, Cécile?"

Cécile opens wide her eyes, that become golden when she is happy. "I adore street fairs! Oh yes, let's go, Henriette—tomorrow, yes?"

"Wait," cries Maurice suddenly, "I'll go along with the two of you, to the fair at Denfert-Rochereau!" Henriette begins to laugh. "Don't you trust me, Maurice?" she asks.

GOING TO THE street fair is the first agreeable event in her life in Paris. Cécile puts on blue jeans and a pullover, she ties her hair behind her neck with a ribbon, making a little ponytail— her head feels so light now, with her hair short. It's odd that Maurice wanted at once to come along—he who never goes anywhere with her during the day. While waiting for him to get ready, Cécile sings herself a little song in the patois of Gascony.

And some money? Suddenly it occurs to her that she has no money—luckily Maurice will be there to pay for her. And the idea comes to her for the first time that Maurice never gives her any money. It's he who pays the rent, the maid, all the household expenses. Cécile never buys a thing; indeed it has never occurred to her to buy a dress for herself, or anything at all. It's the first time in her life in Paris that she's going out someplace where she herself will have to spend some money. For the first time, too, she asks herself exactly what Maurice lives on, how much money he has, are they rich, are they poor? Maurice makes use of cars that are always "his friend's," his apartment is badly furnished, cold, disorderly, but Cécile has attributed all this to the postwar life in Paris; food is rationed, and electricity . . . and her own personal needs have always been so limited that she cannot get any real idea of their situation.

"Cécile, are you ready? Quick, we'll be late," cries Maurice from another room. "We'll pass by and pick up two young fellows, photographers who want to do a reportage on the fair, and we've got to pick up Henriette, and an American." Of course, Maurice would never go anywhere except in a group, Cécile had forgotten; and besides, even the street fair must be exploited, too. One cannot go there simply for fun. Cécile feels her joy in the prospect giving way to sadness.

The two photographers are already there waiting at the corner of the Boulevard St. Germain when the car "borrowed from a friend" comes to a halt. One is young, with gray-white hair, and a pliant form that seems always primed to pounce on some object to be photographed; the other is still younger, he has a melancholy air, his hair is almost long, and he has the voice of a girl.

The gray-haired photographer is full of life; he doesn't stop stirring and moving about, even in the car. He puts his free arm around Cécile's shoulders, with the other he adjusts his camera, he tells risqué stories to Maurice, who laughs his enormous laugh, he crosses and uncrosses his thin legs, he has the car stopped every time he sees a tree, a house, a woman that he wants to photograph, leaping out of the automobile, then, like a devil out of his box, running, crouching, adjusting his apparatus, and returning at a run to the car, to continue his interrupted dirty story, all the while directing Maurice, "Take a right turn, it's shorter that way, no, don't turn there, it's a one-way—"

"Eric," says Maurice, "leave me in peace! Take your pictures and let me drive." Eric laughs goodheartedly. "Good. I'll never give you that book I bought especially for you yesterday—illustrated, old man, something unique."

Another item for Maurice's "special" collection, thinks Cécile, who has made its inventory. The first of these books had been exciting, but read one after another they became disgusting and, worst of all, monotonous.

The other photographer says nothing; from time to time he passes his hand over his hair with an effeminate movement, and sighs. At the entrance to the fair, they find Henriette already waiting, with a young Negro in an American uniform beside her.

"Come on," says Maurice to the two photographers. "I've got an idea for the reportage." Then he turns to Henriette, to the American, to Cécile. "Open your hands, Cécile," he says. "Open them as wide as possible." Startled, Cécile opens her two hands, and Maurice pours a rain of francs into her palms. "Have fun, the three of you, spend it all!"

He has disappeared, and Cécile looks at her hands overflowing with shining coins; she bursts out laughing. All that money! She has never had so much money in her hands.

Already, all around her, the wheels are turning, the swinging chairs mount and descend, the cries of the vendors rise from every side. It is the first postwar street fair, and Cécile feels herself flooded with that same joy that takes hold of her entirely every time the sun shines on her, or when she feels herself free in the great outdoors, surrounded by colors and sounds. The tall American Negro flings himself upon the pleasures of the fair with the very same joy of life that can take such a total hold on Cécile. In him too there is something healthy and animal and indestructible. He is called Eddie, and he is extremely handsome, with a smooth, dark beauty—he has the air of a beautiful, blazing statue emanating its own electricity, confident of its own force. Cécile does not interest him, but he likes Henriette, the cool and solemn Henriette with her hoarse voice, her fierce eyes, her rebellious mouth. For her, Eddie laughs in huge bursts, he sings at the top of his lungs, he sends shooting upward the iron weights that ring a bell before they come tobogganing down—if one has the strength to send them to the top. Henriette watches Eddie and murmurs, "Look at him! He's only a kid, all the Americans are only children, just look how pleased he is to show us his muscles! But you, too, you're only a kid, and I feel so old, with the two of you." She puts her arm around Cécile's waist, with a movement of tenderness. All at once it is no longer her arm but the arm of Mademoiselle that Cécile feels around her waist. The same soft womanly arm. Good Lord, how far away it seems, and yet it was yesterday that she still lived surrounded by women and affection—how she misses all that now—a caress along her throat, her cheek against a woman's breast. And none of the movements that Maurice makes, that burn her, each night, can replace the gentleness of other days. Maurice is heavy, every night on her body, and his shadow seems gigantic on the walls of the room. He talks to her of things that she could never by herself have imagined, it seems to her, and he fills her with himself, only to leave her somehow so empty . . . Here he is returning. Eric leaps along at his side with the bounds of a panther, and the other young man bends his head, still with his air of fatigue, and raises his camera to his face with the movement of a woman who is about to have a look in her handbag.

Maurice throws a rapid glance at Henriette, who still has her arm around Cécile, and at the huge American in uniform, standing in front of them, telling them a story that makes them laugh.

"Well, are you having fun, children?" He comes closer. He too suddenly puts his hand on Cécile's shoulder, a hand whose touch is filled with approbation. Cécile lifts a pair of astonished eyes to him. Since they have been married, this is the first time Maurice has made a gesture of affection toward her, in public. Is it possible that he loves her in some other way than sexually? For how can one love with love, if there is no affection? How has he divined the nostalgia that has just come over Cécile? Or rather, is it a gesture of reward? But for what? What has she done to merit a reward?

AND YET SOMETHING has changed in her life since the fair—Cécile knows that Henriette is her friend. She is no longer really alone in Paris. When Maurice is out, Cécile often escapes from the black apartment, like a fleeing prisoner, and takes the bus to go to Henriette's.

Sometimes Eddie is there too. That he has become the latest lover of Henriette seems evident from the way he looks at her, and Cécile is astonished to feel a sort of jealous contradiction in herself, a jealousy over this big young man, so perfectly beautiful, who has all the rights over Henriette that she—Cécile—could never have.

Eddie doesn't like to talk of America, and if someone speaks to him of it, his eyes half close and his mouth tightens. One day he says, "Henriette, don't ask me questions, you're French, you could never even understand."

"What is it that I couldn't understand?" Henriette insists with her untamed air.

"The ideas that people have in America, about the difference in the color of people's skins."

"Then why are you going back there?" says Henriette.

"Why do you let them do it to you? Leave the place, go back to your own land in Africa, the way the Jews are going back to Palestine—they too were a people who weren't wanted in the countries where they lived. Well then, look—" she reaches out an evening paper to Eddie, with photographs—"Look, there is another illegal ship which the English have stopped. Almost every night there's still another boat full of refugees leaving for Palestine. Why don't you people do the same thing?" Henriette's voice has become feverishly intense: "You have a huge land waiting for you to liberate it, it will be yours! It belongs to all the black people!"

"No," says Eddie, "it's not the same. We are Americans, we like the life there, we want to stay there, only to be equal with other men. But you can't understand it, so shut up."

Cécile is surprised when Henriette keeps on insisting. For herself, she understands that Eddie is marked with too many scars, and that his delirious happiness in living in Paris is a joy that he has kept too long enclosed within himself, and that overflows here because for the first time in his life he feels the intoxication of being free, of being able to sit down wherever he likes, to walk wherever he pleases, to laugh, to love whomever he wants to, and because the eyes of the white people whom he passes in the street look on him only as a man, a man who has a certain color of skin simply as others have a certain color of hair—a human being. Here, he is a human being, and he wants to go home to his own country and be treated like a human being there, too, and not have to begin his life from the beginning, at zero. Perhaps it would need a Hitler in America, and six million black people to be gassed, for the American Negroes, too, to decide to leave everything and begin again in their ancient land.

Cécile hesitates to say this to Eddie. She has always had the greatest difficulty in asking questions of people and in giving them advice. Her instinct is only to look, to observe, and to note things in her innermost being—like a collector. And then, she still feels so inexperienced. How can her judgment have any weight? Eddie treats her like a little sister to Henriette—he smiles to her distractedly, speaks very little to her. Perhaps he after all is also jealous—jealous of her? For Henriette likes to draw Cécile's head down on her knees, to stroke her hair, and Cécile feels herself ready to purr with pleasure under Henriette's hand. With Henriette and Eddie, she goes strolling in the flea market, in the Luxembourg Gardens, and along the quays of the Seine.

Paris is rising slowly from the war. Each day there is more food, there is more clothing in the shops, and fewer things are on ration.

Sometimes as the three of them walk together in the streets, the two girls who look so much alike, except that one is brunette and the other blond, and the big Negro between them, there are people who turn and smile, murmuring, "Well—that fellow certainly can't be bored with himself!"

Nor is Cécile any longer bored with herself now that Henriette is there.

MYETTE IS THERE too. She has disembarked one fine morning, and she is there, with her air of being infuriated by Paris, and even more by the apartment where Cécile lives. She has arrived for a few days, with a little valise in her hand, and no sooner has Cécile flung herself around her neck, than Maurice has vanished, saying, "I must leave you, until tonight then, I have a thousand things to do."

Myette's gaze, so blue and innocent, circles the apartment on the rue Visconti, with its disorder and darkness, and Cécile hurriedly reassures her, "We're looking for another apartment,

Myette, we're only here temporarily, while we wait." As she talks, she hastily closes the drawers, pushed back the piles of newspapers, the photos that might compromise her, terrified at the idea of what Myette might think. "One can't find a thing to rent in Paris, Godmama, you simply can't imagine, so we haven't done much with this place, because after all we're not staying here long, Maurice has several things in view."

Myette enters the conjugal chamber—the huge bed has not yet been made; Myette inspects the bare walls, the faded curtains, and Maurice's clothing scattered everywhere. Her eyes notice everything, particularly the empty vase next to the bed. Aren't there any flowers to be had in Paris? Myette wonders. Everything can be explained, but not the absence of a single flower, a single leaf in this vase. No woman who is happy would keep an empty vase in her bedroom. No matter what the excuses offered by Cécile, Myette looks at the empty vase and understands. Her gaze returns, desolated, to the pale face of Cécile, with her hair cut short.

MYETTE HAS GONE back. At the station, Cécile pressed her forehead for a moment against the warm ample bosom that had served as a maternal breast, the bosom of this woman who had taught her to love that which is indestructible: nature itself.

Now, with Myette, the sun has gone away again; the sun remaining in Paris is only an imitation. Cécile returns to the dark apartment, to her life raft in her bed, to Maurice, to the friends of Maurice, to Henriette.

Henriette sings with fire—and with success. Her face begins to be seen in the press, poets write songs for her, her name becomes a postwar symbol.

It is springtime in Paris. Cécile realizes that this is spring, her first spring in Paris, only because one morning she feels too warm, sitting by the radiator in the salon. She runs with Minou to the window and on the opposite wall she espies a virgin tendril that had looked dead, now digging its tiny green fingers into the dark bricks.

The charwoman has not appeared this morning, and Cécile

begins to leap around the apartment. It's nice out, it's spring, she feels a desire to run, to climb up the trees, to swim in the river, after this long, this interminable winter.

Suddenly Cécile installs herself before Maurice's desk, pushing back the flood of papers that overflows everywhere. She is going to write to Myette and tell her that springtime has arrived here too, even here! That she is happy, that Minou is purring, that she has been to the theater with Maurice and Henriette Arnaud the singer, to see Sartre's latest play, *No Exit*. Cécile pulls a large white sheet of paper toward her, and at the same time an open letter slips down in front of her from under a pile of newspapers; it is an open note upon which Cécile's eyes come to rest, stupefied, because the letters form words and the words form a phrase, "My Maurice, my darling big baby—"

Why does she instantly shut her eyes? Why this fear of reading what follows? Why does her heart begin to thump in huge terrified beats? She feels dreadfully hot and then dreadfully cold, all over her body. And then she opens her eyes, smoothes the sheets with her hand so as to stretch it out quite plainly in front of her, and reads—first the date—quite calmly, she tells herself.

The date is yesterday, and the letter gives Maurice a rendez-vous for the next day, on the rue Gay Lussac at ten o' clock "as usual, my big baby." It is signed Linette. Linette? But that's the name of a dancer in the Folies Bergére, whom Maurice took Cécile to see one day in 1944, when the war was still on.

Cécile looks at the time, on a little round watch that hangs from a chain over her small bosom. It is ten o' clock. Maurice left her, after their breakfast, toward nine, saying, "I have to go to the paper."

Cécile's hand tightens on the letter, creasing it in terror. What should she do?

"As usual, my big baby—" She repeats this idiotic phrase. Is it really possible? How could such a thing have happened? Is it her fault? Because she is too inexperienced to hold a Don Juan like Maurice? Perhaps, then, he is bored with her? She is only a little country girl, after all—how could she know the things that all the Linettes of Paris must know? But then—the things he says to her at night—aren't they true? For how can any word of that be true if she finds this letter from another woman saying "as usual?"

What is she like, that woman? In what is her strength? What is it that draws Maurice to her? Cécile cannot even remember her face . . .

From the courtyard, music mounts, interrupting Cécile's thoughts. Someone is playing an accordion under the window while a companion accompanies the music, singing.

Tu te moques, tu te moques, tu te moques de moi!
Tu crois donc petite sotte que je ne le vois pas—

Cécile rises, she puts on her coat, and goes slowly down the stairs. In the street, she stops a taxi and gives the address on the letter.

All is suddenly tranquil within her. She leans against the cushions of the taxi, she lets herself go with the regular swaying of the ride, and her heart, too, now beats quite regularly. It's strange that she feels nothing, absolutely nothing, but that she watches herself as always, having again become two persons— as though her shadow had once more raised itself up from the ground and set itself to study her.

It is her shadow then that watches her pay the taxi driver, that watches her scanning the house on the rue Gay Lussac, ringing at the door. It is her shadow that listens to her heart begin to thump again, and watches her push against the door, which gives way, opening at once.

Inside the room, Maurice has just turned, and the blond young woman, sitting in her negligee on the bed, has with an astonishing quickness seized hold of a pair of nail scissors, which she clutches in her hand.

Cécile feels neither fear, nor cold, nor warmth. She gazes on the young woman who has got up from the bed. The woman is rather strong, and has heavy breasts. She too does not seem to feel any fright; she holds onto her scissors, but simply with the expression of someone who takes along an umbrella in case of rain. But Maurice sponges his forehead, and the silence endures, until he says in a choking voice, "What a surprise, my dear—were you passing in the neighborhood?"

And Cécile thinks, Of what importance is all this? No, it doesn't even hurt, I don't want it to have any importance, I don't want it to give me pain. With the fury of her age she repeats to herself, I don't want to suffer, and it is in the most polite of tones that she replies, " Yes, I was passing, so I thought I might pick you up, on my way."

Just as quick as Linette was in seizing the pair of scissors, Maurice seizes his hat, precipitating himself toward the door, pushing Cécile out, dragging her into the street. What is he afraid of then? He, afraid? Is one afraid of the dead? Doesn't he know that he has just killed Cécile? This shadow, watching Cécile, could tell him this, since Cécile says nothing; it is so easy for a husband to kill the young girl who was his wife. Such crimes of passion are committed every day. For them to succeed, it is necessary only that the wife be very young, very naïve, and very much in love. But had Cécile been in love?

Until now, had she been asked, she would have said no. That which she feels for Maurice is a tormented passion, it is a physical attraction that dominates her, it is admiration, and sometimes it is fear. But "being in love" is something that one can feel only youthfully, for a boy, she tells herself, it is something at one and the same time light and childish and primitive, it is something that doesn't last. Henriette is sometimes in love, at this moment she is "in love" with Eddie, tomorrow it will be someone else. When one is in love one is jealous, one is unquiet, and Cécile tells herself, I am not jealous—even now, I am not disquieted, Maurice is a man and not an adolescent, he is free. But why this wound in her, this total, annihilating pain?

Standing before the mirror in the entry, she takes off her coat in silence, and gazes at herself in the glass. "Look well," she is told by the shadow that never leaves her, "look well and see what is on this face before you, for one day you'll have need to describe it—this face of death. Examine its landscape, imprint it in your memory, Cécile, one day you will make use of these eyes dilated in pain, these lips pressed tightly one against the other so as not to allow the escape of a single cry."

It's the way of life, Cécile tells herself, life is like that, and it's time that I learned it. She isn't even angry at Maurice. It is her own fault, in having been so naïve, so innocent. That is what has just been revealed to her, and not the infidelity of Maurice. Only the immensity of her ignorance.

AND SHE IS not dead at all. At nineteen, one has a difficult time dying.

It has needed only the night for Maurice to reconstruct joy again in the body of Cécile—like a sculptor rebuilding a statue. His chest under the mouth of Cécile, his arm around her neck, his legs imprisoning the legs of Cécile, and joy is formed anew, as under the blows of a chisel. The other woman—one does not even speak of her, that was nothing, that was only the sort of thing that happens to all men, and is utterly meaningless. And besides, Maurice is an artist, one doesn't imprison an artist in bourgeois conventionality. He must be free and feel free, and the most important thing, above all, is for her to be better for him than all the Linettes of the Folies Bergére—more "sexy" than all the Linettes, more amusing, more daring.

This night, Cécile gives herself to Maurice with a raging thirst, a total abandon—so total that she herself is astonished to be able to give herself like that without shame, without remorse, but determined only to please him, to reconquer him.

But she doesn't "make love," for it is not love that has been in play in this affair. She "has sex" with him, for this is what is in question. Everything is in order, then. Maurice has two distinct roles: he is on the one side a husband, and on the other, sex. Now life can be simple and clear, with each emotion in its proper drawer, with its own regulations, with its special set of reasons.

AND PARIS TOO begins to recognize Cécile. Now one does not speak of Maurice Henry alone, but one says, "And have you seen, have you heard the young wife of Maurice? That extraordinary, that adorable Cécile?"

All the journalists repeat her droll remarks, the painters ask to do her portrait, the café singers make up verses about the Henry ménage, the most in vogue in all Paris. A young film director comes to ask Maurice whether he will consent to have Cécile perform in a motion picture, but Cécile refuses. No, she doesn't want to be an actress, despite the talent Maurice perceives in her. She prefers to have her life free, she likes her long empty days. "I don't know but that you are making a mistake," Maurice says. "Our money is giving out. Films pay very well, and we're broke this month."

It seems, in any case, that they are always "broke." Maurice is forever saying so; he complains continually of a lack of money.

Cécile is sitting on the bed; she has bought a number of ancient glass balls at the flea market and now she rolls them along the bed cover; she is wearing a pair of clinging black trousers and a jersey blouse that molds her small pointed breasts. Maurice contemplates her as he smokes his cigar.

"You know what you ought to do?" he says as he blows a cloud of smoke. "Write a few pages for me about your school in Gascony. Make up a little story, describe the young girls, and the nuns, and Mademoiselle, the loves of Anette, and how the two of you went swimming naked in the river—adolescence is all the rage in literature right now, we might be able to sell it—why don't you try—"

"Oh, no, Maurice, I don't know how to be a writer, and besides, it bores me."

But Maurice has a certain look which Cécile is unable to answer. When Maurice's eyes and face become overcast with that sort of rigid, frozen mask, Cécile feels as if all life is about to flow out of her. "I'll try," she says weakly. "All right, I'll try."

"Don't forget Mademoiselle, your walks with her on the ramparts—and everything," says Maurice, as he leaves the room.

The "few pages" he has asked for somehow turn into an

entire notebook. The next morning Maurice goes off as is his habit, into the mysterious regions of his world, and Cécile, still in pajamas, starts hunting through the crates filled with her father's papers. She doesn't touch the forbidden manuscripts, but she finds a packet of blank white sheets and carries back a thick pile to her room.

What does one do, how does one go about writing a story? She takes a pen, spreads a few sheets on an atlas, and transports everything to her bed. After that, all is easy. It's even amusing. Cécile writes the whole day long, her tongue protruding, her hair in her eyes, and with a smile at the corner of her lips. How should she describe Anette, then? Small and round and dark, as she sees her stretched on the grass near the river, in her wet slip, or with her eyes wide open, repeating "and then? Tell me more, Cécile, tell me more." But in these pages, Cécile will be called Ariane, and Myette will be her mother. There will be neither war nor death. How marvelous it is to be able to create a past for oneself, a past to order.

Now here is Mademoiselle appearing under the pen of Cécile. Mademoiselle, very blond under a wide straw hat, her cheeks so rosy, and with a scent of lavender floating all about her—the scent recalls other odors to Cécile, the chicory-blended coffee, the corridors of the convent at five o' clock, the waxed floors, the starched white curtains . . . the sheets become filled with the round, almost childish handwriting of Cécile. For a whole week, she writes all day long.

She doesn't go to see Henriette, she doesn't answer the telephone. In the evening, Maurice gazes on the mounting piles of paper with satisfaction. And then the week is ended. The story is almost a small novel, there are two hundred and fifty pages of Cécile's writing, and Maurice takes possession of the pile. Cécile goes to brush her hair.

Maurice, sitting in an armchair, reads so quickly—watching him through a corner of her eyes Cécile asks herself how he manages to read what is on a page if he only glances over it? It's true, it's late and they must go to the opening of the Katherine Dunham troupe, come to dance in Paris. Marlene Dietrich will be there, it seems, and Mistinguette, and Jean Cocteaus's latest discovery, the beautiful Jean Marais. "Quick, get dressed," Maurice says, rising and gathering together all the scattered sheets, which he hastily stuffs into a drawer, "I was wrong about your literary gifts, there's nothing to be done with all that scribbling. Well, no matter."

Good, Cécile tells herself. At least now, as far as that goes, I'll be left in peace. The tales of Cécile will again serve for nothing more than the amusement of Maurice's friends, on the long winter nights when the rain beats on the windows of the cafés.

DURING ALL THAT summer of 1946 and through the autumn that follows, Cécile considers that she is making great progress. All Paris says that Maurice's young wife is extremely amusing. The men begin to look at her with a new interest, and the women begin to speak evil of her, as the two things often go together. Cécile goes out a good deal, laughs at all the gatherings, and makes everyone around her laugh when she recounts the tales of her village, with her Gascony accent.

And in the morning when she brushes her hair before the mirror she tells herself, "I've changed, really I've changed."

Before the time of Maurice, her life and her self formed a single whole. Now, her life and her self are composed of tiny pieces, cutouts, as in a puzzle. There is the little piece that still belongs to her past, to her garden, to Myette. There is the little piece that belongs to Maurice, and there is the piece that has almost acquired the shape of worldliness; there is the piece that provides an ambiguous face, for her, and over which all the women keep up their whispering—to her great delight. Little bits and pieces of a complex puzzle which has not yet been fitted together?

The important thing is to be pleasing to Maurice, so that Maurice will not find her too stupid, so that Maurice will not go searching elsewhere for what Cécile doesn't have.

And yet when Cécile, in these highly Parisian evenings, notices Maurice take on a certain air that she has come to recognize, that air of a male in quest of prey, when he inclines himself, then, over some young girl seated on a divan, Cécile's heart becomes altogether contracted. But her anxiety now only makes her laugh more loudly, and concentrate on the first man she encounters at the buffet; her cat's eyes become golden, become dark, become gray, glistening, captivating under their barricade of eyelashes, until Maurice, irritated, refusing to share, leaves his new conquest to come and assert his rights.

And this is a weapon that Maurice has given her, too. Now she knows that there is a way to defend oneself in Paris. She had believed, before—in the ignorance of her days of "before"— that love could do everything, that for the man she would love, love would suffice. The thought had never come to her that masculine vanity nourishes itself on new conquests, and that this vanity is sometimes more important than love.

A woman's most powerful weapon, she discovers then, is the state of emotional independence. And if she is far from possessing this emotional independence, then she must make a pretense of having it. She cannot permit herself to love to distraction, and to show it. She must worry Maurice, to hold him. She must flirt, and have the air of not being too much attracted to him.

And yet, how good it would be to be able to love without afterthought, without tactics, without traps . . .

Oh! It seems to her that she knows so many things, since her marriage. For almost two years, there has unrolled before her eyes this daily extravaganza that at first astonished her, and now sometimes amuses and sometimes saddens her. But if it is now no longer from the height of her perch in a tree that she contemplates the coming and going of the human kind, it is still with the same attention that she fixes her multicolored gaze on the men and women who surround her.

The one being, nevertheless, whom she does not know at all is the one she most wants to know—her husband. She can list his qualities and his faults for herself, but she can never tell the reasons for his faults nor the source of his qualities. Maurice— she sees him living his life, parading himself everywhere, for he adores the crowd, she sees him laboring furiously over his curious task of cutting and assembling all these writings, signing his name to theatrical reviews, novels, gossip columns, plays, and spending more time and energy in bringing these various works into being through all his intermediaries, than if he had written them himself. Maurice—she well knows his cynical attitude, his libertine spirit, his poses, but she also knows his voice in solitude, the one that belongs only to herself, the one that suddenly cracks, and complains of his age, and complains of not being able to write, and worries about losing her. The voice that can make itself tender, and anxious, and pathetic.

To adapt herself to Maurice, to his nocturnal hours of work, to his amusements, to his sexual desires, to his friends—it is to all this that Cécile has given her total energy for nearly two years now.

As for Maurice's infidelities—she tries to get used to them. After Linette, no other letter falling from Maurice's pocket, or left on his desk, could cause Cécile to rush to his secret rendez-vous. Perhaps Maurice had once thought that he married a little provincial, but she will make him change his mind. If he wants to live a bohemian life, and if the hunt for fresh flesh amuses him, Cécile will show him that she is modern in spirit and that she is just as sophisticated as the women of Paris.

Now when they go out to a party, it is Cécile who discovers a pink young face behind the leaves of a potted plant, it is she who motions to Maurice, "Look, over there, Maurice, the tall young brunette, what do you think? How beautiful she is!"

She feels herself less betrayed then, since she is an accomplice.

HENRIETTE IS HER friend, more fully than Anette ever was, or even Mademoiselle. Anette was a fearful little girl, and Mademoiselle was an eternal virgin. But Henriette is a woman, and now it is a woman that Cécile needs for a friend. With Henriette, there is so much for Cécile to say, so much to listen to. And yet she never confides in her about that which most torments her: Maurice. It is so difficult to be the wife of someone who is totally independent, someone whose work suffices for him, above everything else, and who, in addition, lives a secret life all day long, to reappear only at night, and then with exigencies that Cécile believes she must satisfy in order to please him—without even understanding them herself.

Sometimes during the day, solitude, terror, and sadness seize hold of her, in turn. She goes in search of Henriette, then, at her house, in the public gardens, or on the terrace of a café. She never complains. But at times Henriette darts a piercing glance at her and says, "Is something troubling you, my baby? No, you don't have to say a thing, it's as clear as the nose on your face, there's no need for you to blush and to deny it."

Henriette's hand comes to rest then, on her arm, and stays there. It is so knowing, so friendly, so reassuring a hand. Perhaps it would be the simplest of all to solve everything under the hands of Henriette. She would bring Cécile the tenderness which is so lacking to her; this absence of tenderness from which she sometimes feels she will die! And Maurice will have nothing but approval for a liaison that he might, indeed, even find pleasing. Isn't he always pushing Cécile to go and see Henriette? To stay with Henriette, to learn from Henriette? Doesn't he approve of everything that is extravagant and complicated, and besides hasn't he always been persuaded of a liaison in the past between Cécile and Mademoiselle? And doesn't he also suspect her of never having told him the truth in regard to Anette? And at bottom—at the very bottom—is he so mistaken? Evn though nothing of the sort of thing he believes took place, actually happened, in the old days, doesn't Cécile really have an aptitude for feminine love which she has only kept smothered? A tendency that is smothered but that is there, waiting to appear one day, and that Maurice, an expert, has divined?

And how well Henriette knows to caress her, when she is sad. How good it is to rest her head against the long black hair, to laugh too, with Henriette, to dance together with her on some fine afternoon when the air is heavy with scent.

The record turns slowly like some plaintive creature; Henriette gets up, emerges from among the sofa pillows, extending her arms, "Come, Cécile, come dance." Her burning body, against the burning body of Cécile—her eyes, now become so dark—her lips, partly opening—something being born between them—something that is happening . . .

Always, at these moments, the door opens, and Eddie appears suddenly, contracting his brows. Henriette detaches herself and sighs. Cécile hastily says goodbye. "Good Lord, five o'clock already, I must go home!"

Here is the rue Visconti and the dark old house to which she has become so accustomed that she no longer sees its ugliness. Cécile slowly mounts the stairs. Maurice will not be there, he knows she is at Henriette's, and besides, he rarely comes home before dinner. Cécile opens the door quietly, lost in her confused thoughts, in which the long locks of Henriette seem to undulate like seaweed stirring gently in the ocean. Nevertheless, a sound of voices come from the salon; a ray of light streams beneath the door. Is Maurice there, then? Cécile approaches the door and listens. A woman's voice says, "No, no, not here, look, your wife might come home from one minute to the next."

Maurice's voice says, "My wife is a modern woman, she'll understand, don't worry about it."

Is she a modern woman? No, she is not; the tears mount to her eyes, her heart contracts—her heart—but who has the heart to do with all this? This does not concern the heart, this concerns only the sex. Look, Cécile, get hold of yourself, yes, you are a modern girl and Maurice is free and you are going to show him perfectly well that it is true that he is free. This pain in you, your heart that thinks itself breaking—it is simply the idiotic reaction of a little provincial. Are you Anette, to make a jealous scene for your husband? Are you going to make an appearance again the way you did at Linette's, with your eyes staring wide with withheld pain, and your lips trembling—like some drunkard's wife come in despair to the door of a bistro to fetch him home? Ah no, you've changed, Cécile, nobody is watching you anymore, tonight. That other Cécile—you're going to chase her out of your life—you are all by yourself tonight, and you're going to show them all that you are afraid of nothing, that you are a free young woman, entirely modern, a sophisticated young woman who knows what tone to take in every situation.

Cécile sedately opens the door of the salon, smiles to the young woman whom Maurice is pressing to himself, with his mouth on her naked breast.

She advances toward Maurice so quickly that he doesn't even have time to get up. "Excuse me, dear," she says, "I don't want to disturb you, but what should I say to Mme Donoff, she's on the telephone—you know, Mme Donoff, your last week's mistress?"

Maurice stares at her with such astonishment that Cécile bursts out laughing.

"Ah, you imp!" he cries. "What Mme Donoff? You traitor, aren't you ashamed!" He too has ended in a burst of laughter. The lady with the naked breast, blushing furiously, covers her bosom and stutters that she must go. But Cécile won't hear a word of it. "But no, but no, my dear friend, please stay, you must have a drink with us first—it's so cold outside."

THE WOMAN HAS gone, only her perfume lingers, still floating about the salon, a frightfully sweet cheap perfume. Cécile has fled to her room; she gathers Minou up on her bed, hugs her to her bosom and begins to laugh.

A strange joy, savage and evil, bites into her heart. Maurice opens the door, eyes Cécile, and he too starts to laugh, as over some great joke. Cécile's laughter responds, heightened by his own, mounting into a high burst.

In this laughter, Cécile finds something new. She feels herself the victor, and she feels herself for the first time the equal of this man; she is no longer a little girl, nor even a young woman. A young boy, perhaps, with her short-cut hair, and able to share in the adventures of a man.

IT'S RAINING. Maurice is out. Henriette is singing in Madrid, Eddie has gone back to America. Cécile has written a long letter to Myette, and after that, she has straightened out her bureau, fed Minou, and given the dinner menu to the young maid who is working in the kitchen. What else is there to do? It's true that she rarely bores herself, but this afternoon boredom has taken up residence within her. In this weather, she can't even go out for a walk. She doesn't feel like reading, and she has nothing to do. Perhaps, then, it is really the moment, put off for two years, to sort out her father's papers? They are there, in several crates, in the empty bedroom, and for two years Maurice has been repeating to her, "After all, you ought to read these manuscripts, they were never published, and maybe we've got a real treasure in them." But he never really presses her about it; perhaps he doesn't believe that the novels of Cécile's father could be worth anything. All those writers who keep on writing but don't want to show their work to anyone—they must know within themselves that what they write isn't worth the trouble of being shown. Maurice's practical spirit, his acute sense for commercial possibilities in the arts, refuses to accept the idea of a genius truly undiscovered. All right, Cécile tells herself, today or never.

Ever since the day in the winter of 1945 when Henriette's voice said, "You mustn't hope anymore, they are dead," Cécile has kept shut a door within herself—the door that opens on the past, on her childhood. It would have been too painful to reopen that door, too dangerous, too, to permit the reappearance of the two faces that the grownups' war has stolen from her childhood. She has no parents anymore, not a single person from her family, she has only Maurice. He has become her all, her father, her child, her brother, her lover, and her husband—and that is a great deal for only one man. One cannot ask of him also that he love her so much as to fill so great an emptiness—the best is to avoid thinking about that emptiness.

And the war has really receded, 1948 has brought a new prosperity, and new fashions, and an atmosphere of peacetime. One must finally put away all these reminders, eliminate some of them, so as to be able to start again from zero in this postwar world. Maurice speaks of traveling. He has to go to England. To Germany, he has a new film project, he has acquired the rights to a play, a highly sophisticated subject, and there are other new projects . . . It is easier for Maurice to travel thousands of miles and to spend months chasing about one country and another, to fly over the seas, to telephone from one city to another, than to sit down in front of a white sheet of paper and on it with his own hand. Every escape is preferable, to him, to the torture of writing.

"You'll like London," he predicts to Cécile, "it will change you, and we'll come back rich." If she is about to leave, then, she really must finish with this task; she must face these forbidden manuscripts.

It must be cold in that room with the packing boxes. Cécile pulls on a thick ski sweater, and takes along a pillow so she can sit on the floor. She pushes open the door. How dark this room is—like an abandoned tomb.

Once more she hesitates, her heart thumping. What will the voice of her father say to her? Will he bring her a solution? Will she learn what life is, will he give her the key to happiness?

In the first box, she finds only bills, scribbled notebooks, dictionaries, and an atlas.

Another box is filled with school notebooks. How strange—her father had kept all of his classroom notebooks, his grammar exercises, his study reports in geography and history. And old pencils, too, and albums of photographs, menus of restaurants, collections of stamps . . .

Here finally is the box of manuscripts. How the bindings shine, the magnificent leather bindings, fawn-colored, and bottle green, royal blue, garnet—bindings placed on these manuscripts by the hands of her father. His beautiful patient hands, which must have spent so many hours in gluing on the leather, in engraving the titles in golden letters; so much labor, and not this prostitution of words that takes place in Maurice's study.

And Cécile, then, is to be the first person in the world to open these books, and even if they are not masterpieces, what can it matter—the important thing is the love with which these pages have been written. Cécile kneels, like a worshipper before sacred writings, hoping to recover her soul, her faith.

Then she opens one volume, at random, in the middle.

But the page is blank.

Cécile still does not understand. She opens another part of the book, and there too the page is blank.

Her heart begins to thump violently. She takes another volume; all the pages are blank.

Blood mounts to Cécile's face. Is it shame? She looks around her, as though someone might catch sight of her father's lie. His pathetic lie—and his cowardice, too.

All the volumes are empty, hundreds and hundreds of blank pages, not a chapter, not a line, not a word has ever been written.

For years, living on his pension as a war invalid, he had shut himself away, far from his wife and his child, in his study, and he had pretended—but on those days when he had called the child Cécile to him and read her a few verses, a few lines? Were even they his own? Those romantic lines which she can scarcely remember? Or did he perhaps compose those lines in his head, though he never wrote them down?

Like Maurice, then, her father too had an obsession to write but had never been capable of doing it. She was the daughter and the wife of two men suffering from the same disease.

And she herself? Maurice had asked her to write; she had tried and it was worthless—Maurice had told her so. And nevertheless the desolating discovery now raises a strange desire in her, the desire to conquer this disease, to be able to do that which these two men could not do, to prove to them that her youthfulness, her vitality, is stronger than their disease. Perhaps too, in some way, to avenge her father, and prove herself to her husband. To recreate the village in Gascony, the convent, and her youthful years, the face of Myette, the odor of coffee, the sound of Anette's voice, the smile of Mademoiselle—ah! if she could—to recreate them, to make them live forever, to conquer time, to conquer death. But she cannot. Maurice has told her— Maurice knows about writing. Even though he too is unable to write, isn't it his profession to get other writers to work? And she is no writer—not she. He has told her so.

THEN NOTHING REMAINS but to live. To live, totally, to use up the hours, the days, the nights, to taste, to taste with curiosity, with passion—to be just as free as Maurice. All that he can permit himself, and everything that Cécile permits him, she must permit herself too, in order to survive. For Maurice's infidelities are famous in all Paris; people point rather to the woman he has not slept with, than the reverse. And his young wife moves smilingly in the company of this little court of acknowledged mistresses, always indifferent, or polite, worldly and charming. The husbands of Paris praise her to their wives. "Look at Cécile Henry, what toleration, what a modern woman—and you, you make me scenes over nothing."

The scenes are made by Cécile only in her dreams. When she sleeps, when she lets go the reins with which she bridles her jealously all day, there is always the same dream that comes back to torment her. In this dream, she discovers still another new infidelity of Maurice's and she begins to weep, to sob, and she throws herself on him and bites him, she hammers on his chest with her fists, she cries, Why, why? She cannot seem to understand. Gone is her tolerance, then, in her dreams, gone is her patience.

She is sometimes awakened by her own sighs. Then, in the night, she lies wondering at herself, while Maurice sleeps peacefully at her side. Does she then really love him so passionately—to suffer so because he deceives her? But why not tell him, then? Yet the idea of admitting so bourgeois a torment makes her blush in the night.

No, never that. From the beginning of this marriage, she has established Maurice's liberty as a sacred principle. She has accustomed Maurice to seeing her amused and tolerant before his conquests. She has even given him the habit of coming back to tell her of them. It is she who points out his possible victims to him, at the parties they go to, and who discusses their attractive points with him. Doesn't he believe that she is as much an expert on women as he is? And yet she herself has remained faithful to him. No one can speak of a single lover of hers.

Sometimes Cécile tells herself that it is really necessary for her to behave with the same liberty that she gives to Maurice, but she can't make up her mind. Her flirtations are principally with women—with women, there is a warmth, a reassurance—but men make her afraid. Among Maurice's friends, nevertheless, there have been many who were brilliant, who were handsome, and who made all sorts of advances to her, but Cécile has always arranged matters so as to go out with those who, she knows, are not fond of women. With the young men of effeminate manners, she is counted a great friend, and she is often seen in St. Germain-des-Prés, seated at a table with one or two boys who have their own special morality. She listens to their talk, she observes them with her unblinking cat's eyes, registering their confidences within herself. Often Henriette arrives with some new lover, and the café public stares at the wife of the famous Maurice Henry, encircled by the famous nightclub singer with her latest lover, and a notorious pair of pederasts, and then Cécile's moral reputation begins to equal that of Maurice.

Her life has become as agitated as Maurice's, and if her mornings are still calm, given over to the large open bed, to reveries, her afternoons, her evenings are dissipated in the same emptiness, with the same lightness as the cigarette smoke that drifts over the St. Germain cafés.

Of course this life does not satisfy her. To do nothing, to serve for nothing, to be so perfectly useless, could hardly be pleasing to a young woman of her age, choking down within herself her desire to live, her curiosity, her ardor.

If she had a child, she sometimes thinks—but a child could not be a solution, one does not have a child as a cure for boredom, the way one buys a theater ticket, or takes a cruise. And in the atmosphere she lives in, would she know how to raise a child? Is she capable of being a mother, as long as she isn't herself sure that she knows how to be a woman? One may play at living, but one cannot play at being a mother, one may risk one's own life but one cannot risk the life of a child.

Cécile tries, then, to make an occupation for herself. She decorates the gloomy apartment, without taking much pleasure in it. She does Henriette's errands for her when Henriette is pressed for time. She goes to the Louvre to learn something about art, she wanders for hours across the centuries, the styles, the colors and the forms. How lucky they are, these artists so long dead, for they have conquered death in the only way that man knows with certainty. From the depths of the Egyptian centuries, from the depths of the Middle Ages, from the depths of a Flemish or Italian studio these artists emerge to live until our own day. Cécile plants herself before the Victory of Samothrace, so tall, soaring upward from the top of the great stairway, and Cécile, quite diminutive, and all by herself on a weekday, gazes upward upon this stone carved centuries before, and her eyes resuscitate the hand and the soul that sculpted this powerful form, with the fabric pressed clingingly to the body by the wind and the water, the great stirring breath of wind that flows through its wings. Or, still alone, she stands before a small Italian primitive; her marveling eye re-creates the monk who bent with infinite patience over his palette, over his colors as clear and golden as the dawn . . .

They have never died, these painters and sculptors, and they will never die, so long as living eyes rest on their canvases, on their stones. Just as eternity continues through the living eyes that bring life to the poems of antiquity, the verses, the stories, the novels, the speeches of all time . . .

Happy are the artists—immortal.

While as for herself, she is born and she dies like the plants in Myette's garden, blossoming in the sun, and fading one evening, falling again to the ground without leaving a trace of themselves.

BUT WHAT TRULY torments Cécile during these years, more and more, is the devouring hunger for tenderness. Seated in a taxi beside some young pederast who recounts his love affairs to her, or curled with her head on Henriette's knees, or stretched straight in her bed at the side of the sleeping Maurice, it is no longer a sexual desire that torments her, but a hunger for love.

And she has always made a distinction between love and

sex. That which makes her throat tighten, then, and brings tears to her eyes, though the tears never fall, is the longing to find a person who would be a warm refuge for her, an all-enveloping refuge, deep as the arms of Myette, soft as the hands of Mademoiselle, and as strong, as certain as must have been the paternal breast.

Sex she has tasted with Maurice. She knows its bitter taste as she knows its intoxication. She can give herself to Maurice with as much curiosity and pleasure as in the first days of their marriage. Sex is not complicated—neither to give nor to receive. If she wished it, she could have as many lovers as Maurice has mistresses. But this facility in itself bores her in advance, and she knows well enough how little these passing adventures count for Maurice. What she desires for herself is not so much this release of physical tension—that is without importance—and it is not the man of a single night. Stretched on her bed-of-refuge, during the long solitary hours, when the light is going down, outside, she dreams . . .

She dreams of a being that is neither man, nor woman, only two arms that close around her, only a mouth, so warm on her lips, only a body pressed against her own, and she is like an infant, a tiny little infant held in the arms, in the warmth, against the loving breast, enveloped and protected. As it had been during a faraway day in those other times before the war, before the separation, so far off a day in her earliest childhood that the only memory which remains for her is that of hunger.

But can these things be explained to Maurice? Maurice would have neither the time for these childish imaginings, nor the comprehension. Maurice would make love to her, believing himself to be responding to her desire, without seeing that the slender body that stretches itself beneath him cannot be appeased only by these motions of his.

Two or three times, through sorrow, Cécile "tries" another man than Maurice, not by going to bed with him, but in reaching through him for the recomforting tenderness that he may perhaps be able to offer.

Two or three times, at a surprise party, in a car, in a bachelor's apartment, she rests her head on a shoulder, offers her lips, offers her heart, seeking to snatch a breath, a trembling, an animal warmth that will appease her.

But the men who in this way traverse the desert within her believe, each time, that they have to do with a young woman whose husband fails to satisfy her, in the only sense that men know of. Not one then wants—nor can be contended with— tenderness. If Cécile is nether unsatisfied, nor frigid, then she must simply be a tease. What is she doing in their arms—this young woman with a child's face, who offers her mouth and refuses her body?

And Cécile too asks this of herself, or rather her shadow asks it, her shadow that notes down the scene, that listens to the beating of her heart, that observes the face of the man leaning over her mouth. That face, which each time in turn also covers itself with the same rigid mask, the mask without eyes, the mask that covers an enjoyment that is solitary and remote, this same mask that Cécile perceived long ago on the face of Maurice in the garden of a little town in Gascony.

In this way she tries one, or another, like some ingénue who is believed to be a libertine. She tries, and searches, and never finds.

ONLY THE GRIPPE could have laid Maurice low; he is in bed, furious, fretful, feverish. Cécile runs from the kitchen to the bedroom, fetching cups of tea, medicines, inhalations. Maurice is the sort of invalid who demands constant attention. He takes his temperature every five minutes, and flops about his bed like a fish out of water. "Good Lord! And that meeting I had set up with Biel—I'm going to miss it. And my piece for Friday— Lorient was supposed to do it for me and he'll never have it ready in time if I don't push him! Cécile, bring me the file on that play at the Ambigu. Cécile, where is my pen? Cécile, I'm dying of thirst! Cécile, open the windows. Cécile, give me that pile of papers, there, on my desk."

Red-faced, agitated, furious, Maurice curses the grippe and falls into despair. It's the first time in ten years that he's had to stay in bed in the middle of the day, and for his temperament this is as bad as a year in prison.

Cécile fetches him the pile of papers from his desk and Maurice turns the sheets, makes notes, erases, wipes his nose, drinks tea, groans, all simultaneously. His heavy, powerful body turns over, suddenly, beneath the covers, and everything, the sheets, the eiderdowns, the papers—everything falls to the floor.

All at once while Cécile gathers up the scattered papers and hands them back, Maurice exclaims, "Look—your reminiscences—I thought I had thrown them in the wastebasket." He picks up the sheets, rearranges himself in the bed, leaning against a pile of pillows. "Cécile, bring me a pencil."

He reads now in silence; gradually this strange quiet invades the room. Worried, Cécile wanders around the chamber. What is the cause of this concentrated look on Maurice's face, while he reads these pages she wrote—it must be two years ago. Hadn't he decreed, then, that all this was worthless? And why hadn't he destroyed this bundle of papers, as he had said he would? But Maurice says nothing more. He contracts his brows, and reads without uttering a word. Each page as it is finished is set down next to him on the bed. A half-hour passes. Cécile has put the room in order, she has gone out, she has returned, Maurice still reads. Cécile senses the approach of some danger. She doesn't really know why. It is like when Myette in the old days would look at a calm sky and announce, "It's going to rain, take in the chairs from the garden," and five minutes later black clouds would appear in the sky. In the same way Cécile watches Maurice's face and tells herself that something is going badly. And here is Maurice lifting his eyes, at last, from the pile of pages in his hand, and looking at Cécile. "What an imbecile I am," he says. "But it's very good, what you wrote here! Of course it needs to be revised, corrected, but it will be publishable, I even think it will sell very very well. You are going to get to work right away, and first make some notes about how you are going to fix this for me."

"But Maurice, I'm too lazy, and besides you told me yourself it was no good. You're feverish and that's why it seems different to you now, wait until tomorrow, you know perfectly well that I can't write."

"Ridiculous!" cries Maurice. "Everybody can write. All that you need is for someone like me to help you. By yourself, I don't say you can, but if I explain to you what you have to do, there's no reason why you shouldn't manage it, and besides we have no money, we're broke again, you'll have to get right on it. You're going to fix up these stories about Anette, lesbianism is in fashion right now, I want some suggestive scenes, that's what sells the best—something scabrous, plenty of sex, some amusing lines, a little perversity—from now on you're engaged as one of my collaborators."

It is in this way that, despite her protestation, Cécile is obliged to go back and start writing again.

A FEW DAYS later Maurice comes home earlier than usual and finds Cécile on the divan, with her cat and a novel.

"What!" he cries. "Is this the way you work?" Suddenly there is that light in his eyes, that strange flicker as in the eyes of Minou when her hair rises at the sight of another cat, and she is about to jump at its throat. Cécile crouches back inside herself.

"Come on, follow me," Maurice says in a dry tone. Cécile gets up and follows him, without understanding. Standing in front of his desk Maurice says, "Sit down." With a sweeping movement he clears the desk of a mess of papers that fall to the floor. Maurice sets the pages Cécile had written on the desk, adds some blank white sheets, and a ballpoint pen.

"Now write," he says. "I'll come and get you—" he looks at his watch—"in four hours. And remember everything I told you. If there are places where you don't know what to do, leave blank spaces and I'll fill them in later."

On this last word, Maurice goes out, and Cécile hears his key turning, with a curious definitive sound, in the lock of the door.

A prisoner. She is the prisoner of Maurice, until her task is completed!

Cécile bends over the white pages; she tightens her hand on

the pen; she begins to write, for she is frightened, and the only way to calm her fear is to write, as he demands.

When Maurice's key turns in the lock four hours later, he finds a quarto of paper nicely filled.

Cécile believes herself free, and is already rising to flee, but Maurice stops her. "Wait," he says as he glances through the pages. They dutifully carry out the corrections he had noted on Cécile's first effort. "Yes, it's not bad, my little one," he finally says at the end of a long moment, while Cécile stands watching him with a worried air. "Yes, yes, it will do for today, but tomorrow, at the same time, you'll be here, and you'll continue."

His satisfied air ends by making Cécile laugh. So now she has a new way to please Maurice. All she has to do is write, to write as he wants her to, and Maurice will continue to love her. Isn't this simple, and wonderful? Of what had she been afraid?

BUT ON THE next day, when Maurice with the punctuality of a jailer comes to free her at the end of four hours, he is less satisfied as he reads her efforts. For several pages Cécile, carried away by her yesterday's happiness, has let herself go into quite a flight of poetics. Maurice seizes a red pencil, slashing and slashing. "Not so much sentiment, it's too romantic. More sex. What we need is a suggestive novel."

Cécile lowers her head guiltily and remembers with a strange feeling of incredulity the little girl of long ago who planted herself before her father and decreed—she too—"It's too romantic, Papa."

"AND TO THINK that I could have failed to notice it! That I could have walked right past such a gold mine, a natural talent—I—and never even sensed it! Of course she needs to be guided, corrected, disciplined, but she has the main thing, the ability to sit down in front of a blank sheet of paper and let her pen run on, without a bit of fear—to let herself go, to obey her instinct, to jump in. She can jump all right, she hasn't got the paralysis by which her father suffered—and I too. Who would have believed it? That little Cécile—she always manages to astonish me. What has she got hidden behind that round forehead, behind those eyes—still so pure—and behind those lips, so perverse? This child-woman that I never manage to capture . . ."

AFTER THREE YEARS of marriage, after two months of labor, locked in for four hours each day, with Maurice repeating in every possible variation, "Hurry, hurry, my little one, we're broke," Cécile at last completes the final approved pages of her first novel.

Maurice seizes the block of paper, writes on the front sheet *"Pas Encore la Jeunesse,"* and nods his head. "Yes—it'll be a good title." He closes the folder, then opens it once more. Peering over his shoulder, Cécile sees him adding two words under the title: "by Maurice Henry."

Of course an author's name is necessary, and doesn't Maurice sign all the products of his factory?

Cécile doesn't get disturbed over so small a matter, and finally freed from her prison, she slips away to recover her peace on the sofa, with the warmth of the radiator, and the purring of a contented Minou.

Afterward there come months and months of vacation. Nothing really happened. Maurice doesn't shut her in under lock and key, indeed Cécile and he make a short voyage to London, and then another to Copenhagen. Henriette is getting a collection of songs ready for a tour in America. Everything is normal—in the summer, Maurice is seen at the races in Deauville, accompanied by a laughing, docile Cécile and some new "lady friend" of the moment. The winter is spent in Paris, at cocktail parties and dinners.

Nothing at all, nothing until morning when Maurice receives a package brought by a messenger, opens it and calls Cécile. "Come, have a look, this will amuse you."

Cécile approaches and opens her mouth wide. *"Pas Encore la Jeunesse"* she reads on a book cover, "by Maurice Henry."

"Here, look—it's nicely got up, eh?"

Cécile holds out her hand, takes the slender volume, opens it, and begins to read the phrases that sound so familiar to her.

". . . Anette placed her blond head on my shoulder. Gently, I stroked her neck, 'Anette, do you love me? Do you love your Ariane?'"

"Oh, Maurice, it gives me such a strange feeling! It's really been published—this book! I thought that you had once more forgotten it!"

"Ah, that, no! I don't make such stupid mistakes twice! In a week this book will be in the stores, in two or three weeks we'll see the reviews, but it's going to be a success—I'm sure of it. There's already a film company interested. Tomorrow I've got to talk to Vadim—and then, I have an idea for getting a play out of it, and Henriette will play the part of Ariane . . ."

And, in short, there is a total, lightning success. Between one day and the next, Maurice has become the author of the celebrated memoirs of Ariane, the little country girl from Gascony who tells the most deliciously suggestive tales in *Pas Encore la Jeunesse*.

At all the parties, now, Maurice often repeats, "My wife's recollections obviously were a great help to me, for years she's been recounting these stories, we really have no idea what goes on in France . . . ."

Cécile at bottom is content that nobody knows it is she who has written the book. She is a little ashamed of it. It doesn't seem too good for her, she would rather that Myette should think it is really Maurice who wrote it. All those suggestive stories—it's embarrassing. The only good part is that Maurice is satisfied, that he doesn't complain about being broke, and that he has generously even established an allowance of pocket money for Cécile. "Here, take this, go buy yourself a dress, some perfume, whatever you like."

A Parisian theater is going to perform a play adapted from *Pas Encore la Jeunesse* by still another of Maurice's colleagues "in collaboration" with him. After that, the film rights will be sold, and in both Henriette will play the part of Ariane. Already, all of Paris knows that Ariane is Cécile herself, and that Henriette is the very image of Cécile.

Besides, Maurice no longer goes out except with Henriette and Cécile together, and the trio causes gossip in the papers and provokes a chain of ever more scandalous publicity. "All the better," says Maurice. "This helps sell the book, it raises anticipation for the play; the more publicity the better." He slips his arm through that of Henriette's on one side, and the arm of Cécile on the other. "Let's go to the races, we've got to show ourselves, all this is wonderful!"

Besides—Cécile finds a good deal of amusement in the shocked air with which people look at them, After all, there is no reason for them to be shocked.

Maurice has arranged to take out still another producer tonight, an American producer—Daryl Zanuck, "Quick, Cécile," he cries the moment he gets inside the door, "it's important. I'm going to try to sell him the film rights to *Pas Encore.*"

While he dresses, Maurice enumerates the characteristics of the celebrated producer, his extravagant life, his talents, his films. At the end, he says, "Put on trousers, and we'll go to the Monocle. That will amuse Zanuck."

And so it is that Cécile has once more been enlisted in the game, seated at a table between the two men. But as it happens, she rarely remains seated, as the official lesbians of the cabaret come in turns to ask her to dance.

It isn't much fun, because almost all of them are masculine, harnessed in their black tailored suits, with neckties, and flat-soled shoes, and they are not at all gay in their bar-girl roles. Cécile is fond of frail women, blond and pliant, perfumed—or else untamed and black like Henriette, with her long hair scattered on her shoulders, and her eyes of a tigress. But what interest can there be in these women, most of them without a touch of charm, travesties of men—and of ugly men to boot—with their heavy voices that they insist on making growly, and their professional manner of dancing. Nevertheless it's curious. Maurice and Zanuck, installed behind their glasses of Pernod, wear an air of satisfaction and amusement. They have the feeling of participating in something authentic and very very vicious.

Cécile feels sad, as always when she deceives Maurice. She would like to get out of this nightclub, to press herself against Maurice, to tell him, "I don't like it here. Take me far away, far from people; the whole world lies, I'm afraid of big cities, afraid of your friends, I want to recover my innocence and the scent of the dawn, I want to hear a thousand sounds in the countryside . . . I'm only myself, happy and free, in the world of nature. I don't like to play the extravagant woman, I don't want to play at all anymore, only I don't know how to end this game."

But how is it possible to avow these things to Maurice without risking losing him? Cécile asks for another drink, and smiles at one of the "bar girls" and gives herself up again, following her onto the dance floor, with a wink at Maurice.

Zanuck has a small blond mustache and a Chaplinesque smile. Cécile, back at her table, puts both hands over her ears; then the entire room takes on a Chaplinesque appearance too—the women dancing, the clients leaning forward, leaning back, the female orchestra, the singer behind the microphone, opening and closing her mouth like a fish out of water—all of it bathed in acrid smoke that stings the eyes, brings up tears, and makes you cough.

"How sad—an evening of fun," thinks Cécile, discouraged, "as sad really as a life of fun."

THE BIG SENSATION of this Paris season at the end of 1948 is a young American who gives up his passport at the Embassy and proclaims himself a Citizen of the World. Cécile avidly reads the accounts in the press, and Maurice even takes her to hear Garry Davis at the Salle Pleyel, one night of torrential rain.

"I have an idea," says Maurice, "a film in which this young idealist will be the hero, a modern Don Quixote—I'm going to talk to some producers about it."

Always and in everything there is Maurice's spirit of practicality and his way of exploiting every encounter for his own ends.

So it happens that Cécile encounters a redheaded young American, in Maurice's office, at a dinner in Camus's, at a press conference.

He is the second American she has come to know since the end of the war—the first was Eddie. Both are young and ready to fight for their ideas. But Eddie believes in a struggle of violence, and Garry believes in a passive struggle, in the manner of Gandhi. Their aim is nevertheless the same. It is the aim of unity: all men are equal and have the right to be free. There is no difference between men, no matter what their color, no matter what their nationality.

How simple it is and how self-evident. Isn't it unbelievable that it should be necessary to fight to prove and to establish something so fundamental, so normal?

It is as though one had to fight to prove that all men have two eyes and one mouth, fight to establish the right to breathe, for all men without exception!

And yet this insane world, this lying world in which Cécile lives in the company of millions of other humans, has not, in the two or three million years of existence on this terrestrial planet, established this essential right for all men.

For Maurice it is nothing but a matter of film, a good subject to make use of. Cécile's enthusiasm for the movement that is growing around the young American pilot amuses him as much as her indignation, in the past, when she came home from Henriette's, preoccupied with Eddie's bitter tales of his experiences.

Maurice can only say, "What a child!" It is the exclamation with which he generally resolves all that irritates or intrigues him in Cécile.

Nevertheless, at the cocktail parties and the soirees, at the first nights, Cécile often falls silent now, withdrawing to a corner of the salon, and asking herself questions. The brouhaha around her doesn't distract her at all. It is so easy to withdraw into oneself, to make a refuge for herself there, even when some guest approaches to recount a worldly bit of gossip, while Cécile, her eyes fixed on him, hears nothing, smiles politely, as she thinks about Eddie, perhaps at this same moment being driven out of a restaurant or a bus in the south of the United States, or of Garry carrying on a hunger strike, sitting atop the debris at the Franco-German frontier.

Is there no way then in which she can help them? No, nothing, really, and her uselessness, her incapacity, brings tears to her eyes. She is nothing but an unknown young woman. All she has been able to do is write an insignificant little novel that doesn't even carry her own name on it, a little bastard of no importance whatsoever. Her life is totally futile, and has nothing to bring to anyone and will never resolve anything for anyone.

And yet if she were a writer, a true writer—what power her pen could have, what influence on men. Like the pen of Zola, like the pen of Victor Hugo—fighting to combat injustice.

Yes, Maurice is right. She is nothing but a child. And a child is incapable of nothing.

IT'S TO ST. TROPEZ that Maurice takes Henriette and Cécile in the summer of 1949. He has had a great publicity idea. He buys them exactly identical bikinis, the same cotton pants, the same long dresses—and on the beach, at the races, at the casino, at the hotel bar, he now appears accompanied by the two young women who look alike, who dress alike, and about whom all Paris and all St. Tropez are talking.

St. Tropez is still a village, a village on the eve of dying as a village and being reborn as a fashionable beach resort. In the calm little lanes, on the terraces of the two or three cafés, among the last authentic fishermen, there begins an infiltration of a few painters, a few celebrities, like Maurice, like Henriette. A nightclub has opened, and it attracts the summer residents of Cannes, of Juan-les-Pins, who drive up after dinner, though they still return to their habitats at dawn when the village awakens, as yet intact.

Maurice, however, scents the air of St. Tropez and issues his decree: What a charming place! It's much better then Antibes, much better than Villefranche—the time has come to launch St. Tropez!

Already a few journalists have appeared, clicking their cameras at Henriette and Cécile, whose identical wardrobes Maurice has further enlarged with identical sets of white linen Corsaire pants, and identical sailor's jerseys in blue-and-white striped cotton.

Maurice halts in their promenade along the quay, poising one hand on the left shoulder of Henriette, and his other on the right shoulder of Cécile. He smiles without taking the cigar out of his mouth. "Yes," he remarks, then, to the reporter from *Paris Match*, "I'm promenading my children, as you see, my two daughters." And he starts laughing. "I'm fond of having them dress the same way, like twins, they resemble each other so, and besides, they can't bear to be apart—these children."

Cécile blushes under her tan, and Henriette turns her head aside. But Maurice has decreed, "It's publicity. We all need publicity. Henriette, your name has to be in the papers all the time, even if in a scandalous way, that doesn't matter at all. And my name, too—people musn't stop talking about the creator of Ariane—our second volume will come out next winter." For Cécile has written a second volume, a sequel to *Pas Encore la Jeunesse.* The background and characters were suggested to her by Maurice, who then again kept her under lock and key every day until the complete manuscript was delivered to him. Since then he has revised, corrected, ordered a few additional chapters. He is a pitiless master of style, and when it comes to making Cécile write, he has absolutely no sympathy nor will he make concessions. "Take that out for me, idiot, the paragraph at the beginning should come here. Cut—enough, no more descriptions . . ." His notations fill the margins, biting and quick, like the strokes of a whip.

St. Tropez, then, is a reward, a well-earned rest, and now Maurice, satisfied, discusses Henriette's role with her, for she will play Ariane this winter, as soon as the season opens.

When the two young women are alone sometimes, stretched

on the beach in their identical bikinis—pink, with white eye-lets—stretched on the hot sand, abandoned at the edge of the sea for a few moments by Maurice, under the crushing mid-day sun, Henriette asks, "But Cécile, these books—it's you who writes them, why don't you sign them?"

"Shh!" cries the frightened Cécile. "Not so loud. If someone should hear you! It's a secret that I write them, and without Maurice I would never have written them, I would be incapable, you know that perfectly well. He helps me, tells me what I should write, corrects me, it's much more his work than mine, and besides I wouldn't even want to sign these books, I don't find them so good, and my own name doesn't mean anything, no publisher would want me, the name of Maurice is famous, that's something else."

"I don't know," says Henriette. "It seems to me stupid to reason that way. If it sells well, it would sell just as well if it was signed by you."

"That's because you don't know anything about publishing," says Cécile, "and besides, if Myette thought that I was writing such scabrous things, it would be terrible for her. No, I much prefer that it should be Maurice who signs them."

"And above all," says Henriette, picking up a fistful of sand and letting it run through her fingers, "you love him in such an idiotic way that whatever he tells you to do, you do. He tyran-nizes you—"

"No, that's not true," protests Cécile, "he doesn't tyran-nize me, I'm just too lazy. I'd a thousand times rather do what Maurice wants than rebel—it's so much more simple to let him decide."

"How much a woman are you," says Henriette, "how docile by nature you are, toward the man you love. I—I would revolt ten times a day in your place. I would rather command than obey. I prefer to play the role of the man." She gets up and reaches out her hand. "Come, let's go swimming."

The sea is warm. Henriette, followed by Cécile, puts a dis-tance between herself and the shore; her long hair floats around her, her shoulders are muscular and sportive. More quickly tired despite her country upbringing, Cécile gasps, "Not so far, Henriette, I'm out of practice." Henriette turns back, and pulls Cécile's arms around her neck. "Come on, swim with me, I'll hold you." Their two bodies, supple, bronzed and salty, glide along, one against the other, like two fish; Henriette's arm encircles the shoulders of Cécile, their legs intermingle amid the waves, their blond and black hair is wetted together. Cécile closes her eyes; a strange happiness invades her, seems to flow through her entire body; words of poetry from other days come back to her memory:

> J'avais ta chevelure autour de mon cou . . .
> Je les caressais et c'etaient les miens
> Et nous étions liées pour toujours ainsi
> Par la meme chevelure, la bouche sur la bouche . . .

She opens her eyes. The mouth of Henriette has a seashell taste, on her mouth.

MAURICE IS ON the beach, and he looks at them for no more than a second, beneath half-closed eyelashes, when they come out of the water, their arms enlaced, he smiles.

"I'M LEAVING YOU here," Maurice declared that same evening. "I'm going by car to the casino in Nice—they say that Orson Welles has just arrived on the coast and I want to see him about a project. Amuse yourselves without me. Wait—here's some money." He hands a packet of bills to Cécile. "It's possible I won't be back until dawn, don't get worried."

He has gone off. He's given them the night, the whole night.

"Let's go for a walk," says Henriette. "Let's go as far as the port, and take a boat."

By habit, they have already put on the same blue jeans, the same pullovers with turtleneck collars. In the boat, Henriette takes the oars. While the vessel slowly moves away from the shore in the moonless night, she begins to sing in her low hoarse voice, for Cécile alone.

Si tu t'imagines,
Fillette, fillette,
Si tu t'imagines
Qu'ça va, qu'ça va
Qu'ça va durer toujours
La saison des amours . . .

Cécile stretches out in the boat, places her head on Henriette's knees. Her upturned face offers itself to the star-filled firmament; happiness fills her, she is choking with happiness. She feels herself become part of this night, the stairs, the sky, the splashing of the water around the boat, part of that hoarse voice that cradles her, part of the perfume of Henriette, part of the body of Henriette. It seems to her that such happiness, so total, so pure too, has not taken possession of her since the hours of long ago in her garden in the dawn, in the solitude of Myette's garden. In this night, it is as though she had rediscovered her childhood among the women and the verdure, the piercing laughter of Anette and her little body naked and round, the arm of Mademoiselle, so light around her waist, the scent of rose bushes, the taste of the dew—all this, and in addition, added to all this tenderness, an animality, primitive and violent, that mounts in her too and that makes her desire the mouth and the body of Henriette, as though famished. We have all night, she thinks, a whole night that Maurice has offered us. What she had been waiting for so long—will she find it now?

She thinks of Maurice first without remorse and only with a kind of gratitude—hasn't he permitted her Henriette? But if he had thought that Henriette was really her first woman, would he still have permitted this? Has she not deceived him with her emancipated airs, her modern ideas, the liberty she has allowed him? If he knew that Cécile was atremble with ignorance and happiness at the same time with the arms of Henriette closed around her in the little fishing boat, would he still have been so generous? Hasn't Cécile been playing this game for him since that evening on the ramparts with Mademoiselle?

And then she doesn't think anymore . . . the vessel drifts in the lee of the wind . . . Henriette's hands have a never-known gentleness, her hair has the scent of vanilla, her shoulders are still salty, the brown point of her breast is like a tiny shell poised on a small white rock.

IT'S ALREADY FOUR years since the end of the war. From her holidays, Cécile has brought back so many remembrances within herself, of beauty, of tenderness . . . The sea, the beaches of the Midi, two adolescents wandering in a wheatfield, holding hands, the hoarse voice of Henriette singing in a fishing boat at night, the aged courtesans ending their lives in the sun on the Promenade des Anglais at Cannes, the faces of women at the casino, the fish jumping in the blue nets on the quay . . .

It is difficult to get used to Paris again, to her life in a cage, to the cocktail parties.

As soon as they are back, Maurice puts her to work. "While we have the play from the first and second books on this winter, we mustn't lose any time, my little one. Write me a light little romance—wait—something taking place at St. Tropez, use your remembrances, I hope you took some notes this summer—a young couple, the story of a young couple, very modern—a triangle—invent me an original triangle . . ." It's strange—she writes to please Maurice, without enthusiasm and without revolt, but with the application of a pupil who wants to attract the attention of the teacher she loves. She writes without difficulty because to write has never been either a passion or a mission for her. If Maurice had insisted that she sing or dance she probably would have set herself to it with the same ease. Myette, had she ever married, would have spent hours in concocting fine dishes for her husband, in creating a magnificent garden for him—it is just as natural for Cécile to try to please through her writing.

The success of her first two books doesn't go to her head, for she herself has difficulty in realizing that it is really she who has written them. Anonymity makes her modest, and she has ended by almost believing that it is truly Maurice who is the author. Besides, isn't it Maurice who had the idea for these books, who pointed out the scenes to her, who revised the passages that displeased him, and above all who so often repeated to her, "Och! What would you do without me! It would be impossible to publish such stuff. Luckily you have me to revise all this. You have a good style, my little one, and facility, but writing a book that sells—that's something else."

And Cécile is quite in agreement. Yes, luckily she has him—for to have Maurice is also to have him there, to have his approbation, his smile, the caress, even if distracted, of his hand, to have his powerful body, a magnificent body, heavy against her own slight form. In the arms of Maurice she feels herself small and protected, sheltered from this worldly, mocking, cynical Paris.

So she tells herself quite often that she is happy like this, and she writes it quite often to Myette, to reassure her, and she repeats it to Henriette if Henriette questions her about her life.

Yet nevertheless the wound is there, that tiny wound, scarcely visible at the beginning, so deeply hidden—the wound seems still to be there and to grow. Is it because of the infidelities of Maurice, more and more frequent? Is it because of his indifference? Is it her wasted life in Paris? Is it the thought that she is capable of nothing by herself? Is it because of Henriette, whom she doesn't see as often as she would wish?

In their new apartment on the quays to which they have moved, she has set herself to write this third novel, taking place in St. Tropez. Cécile has a study all to herself, and a splendid Louis Philippe desk that Maurice has bought at the flea market. Through her window she watches the flow of the Seine and the yellowing of the chestnut trees, and the fall of rain or of snow.

Maurice no longer needs to close her in under lock and key—she has learned to obey. Maurice fetches her a pile of white paper, a new ballpoint pen, and tells her, "Get yourself set, write me two chapters, I'll be back to look them over at three o'clock," and he disappears.

Afterward, she puts on a woolen dress and a camel-hair coat, she winds a Scotch plaid scarf around her neck and head, and she goes off to Henriette's.

To complete the daily chapter imposed on her by Maurice has become the key to paradise—and paradise is Henriette. To be free has come to mean to be free to go to Henriette's.

Must she forever be unable to love without passion? Can't she then learn to love like the rest of the world? To "be in love" in small doses? The way Maurice loves his various mistresses, for a week or for a night; the way Henriette loves her lovers—laughingly, without taking anything seriously? And this too torments Cécile in her relationships with Maurice and Henriette: won't they become tired of her, as they tire of everything?

As for Maurice, it seems to her that so long as she writes what he wants her to, and so long as she plays at this game of appearing emancipated and amusing for him, of seeming avid and curious and ready for anything, he will be interested in her. With Henriette it is something else. Henriette knows her much better. Henriette knows that Cécile is innocent and frightened. A woman lies with much greater difficulty to another woman than to a man. That is why women are often severe with each other, to the incomprehension of their men. Women, among themselves, know each other as no man can know them.

But for the moment, Cécile's innocence is pleasing to Henriette. Henriette likes the notion of protecting and instructing her—this twenty-two-year-old child who is as ignorant as "a little Tahitian before the arrival of the missionaries," as she sometimes laughingly remarks, quoting a phrase from Mr. Willy, the famous Parisian boulevardier of the turn of the century.

The new novel Cécile is writing takes form little by little. It's strange, this act of writing. When she begins, Cécile knows only vaguely where she is going. Each chapter is a small part of a puzzle, explaining nothing to her in itself. She doesn't as yet even see what her book is about. And then when there are enough small pieces set one alongside the other, an image at last appears, and Cécile, astonished, sets herself to reading it all, and begins to understand what is taking place in this novel of hers. The characters too arrive like unexpected guests at a reception. She welcomes them, brings them in, and little by little finds out about them so as to come to know who they are.

In this new novel, there's a character invited by Maurice. It's the husband. Cécile has opened the door to him, he has come in. Cécile doesn't particularly like him; she doesn't even like his name—Frederic. He is too vague, too unreal. It's as though she can't manage to understand a husband, as though the notion of a real husband is too unknown to her. Frederic is a sort of mirage of a husband, too tender, too attentive, a sort of American actor with teeth too white, who smiles too often. And yet how comforting he is for Cécile. When Maurice commands, "To work! Come—yesterday you wrote me only a single chapter, I want four today," and when his eyes take on that dark flicker that makes Cécile shiver with fear, how comforting it is then for Cécile to open her manuscript, to open the door, and to snuggle her new heroine, Juliette, in the reassuring arms of Frederic.

AND HENRIETTE, TOO, has a great success—in her part as Ariane. After the agitated weeks of rehearsals and the opening, the play has settled into a sort of agreeable state of success. The newspapers and the magazines have interviewed Maurice Henry, the author of the novels from which the play has, with his collaboration, been adapted. Photos have appeared of Henriette—accompanied by Maurice—but the magazines have specialized above all in pictures of Cécile dressed exactly like Henriette, of the two of them together at St. Tropez, at the races, of Cécile in Henriette's dressing room, with Maurice always in the background, smiling, with his eternal cigar, presenting his twins to the world with a little amused glint. When the three of them go out together in Paris, even the most sophisticated of Parisians whisper as they look at them. At the exhibit of the fashionable young painter Bernard Buffet, all the heads turn with single movement, as at the races when the horses come into sight running neck and neck—so it is when Maurice enters, one arm in Cécile's, the other arm around Henriette's waist. The crowd smiles and people whisper politely behind their fans or their catalogues, "Look, my dear, explain to me, exactly who sleeps with whom in this ménage of the Henrys?"

"It's odd—they really look alike, it's not only a legend."

"It seems that it's Henriette who wrote *Pas Encore la Jeunesse*."

"Why, no, it's Cécile Henry, didn't you know? All Maurice did was sign his name to it."

But Carmen Tessier, the gossip of *France-Soir*, has given assurance that Maurice himself wrote the two novels, using his wife's remembrances. "It's a book written by a man—this stares you in the face."

At the entrance to the gallery, Henriette suddenly hesitates. "No, Cécile, I've had enough. Everyone is staring at us. I've had enough of this sort of publicity. I'm not going out again as a trio."

Maurice pushes her gently and firmly forward, with the flat of his hand against the small of her back. "Look, Henriette, don't act like a convent girl, you've been through this before, this little sensational entrance is worth twenty mentions in the press for us tomorrow, and months more for the play."

Cécile herself has already gone in and has planted herself before a painting, with a glass of champagne in her hand. She is less embarrassed than Henriette, perhaps more innocent. And besides, it has always amused her to shock people. How she used to laugh, running through the streets of her little village without a hat, without gloves, with her socks falling around her heels, watching delightedly out of the corner of her eye as the curtains behind certain windows stirred with her passing, and imaging for herself the pinched look on the face of Mlle Angelique, and the faces of the other old maids and matrons. "That Cécile! What a tomboy! She'll surely turn bad!"

It was a game, and later she had begun another game—to shock even Maurice, to recount the most astonishing tales to him, to startle a man like Maurice! The game had continued in Paris—always to astonish Maurice, to go with him to the Monocle in slacks, and to get herself asked to dance, there, with all the special entertainers, to flirt outrageously at parties until he came over to put an end to it, and now to flaunt her liaison with Henriette.

Cécile approaches Henriette, and offers her her own champagne glass. Henriette hesitates for an instant, but it is a challenge, and her black eyes at once become savage. She likes to be challenged, she isn't afraid of a soul. She bends her lips to the glass held by Cécile. Maurice smiles. The crowd has again begun to whisper—people are busier looking at the Henry "ménage" than at the paintings. But that's normal. Nobody looks at paintings at the opening of an exhibition.

AT THE LATEST fashionable nightclub, Carole's, there is a new sensation, a singer who is actually a little Negro dancer, a girl who has departed from Katherine Dunham's ballet troupe to become the sexiest, the prettiest singer in Paris—Eartha Kitt.

The habitual clients, and the tourists and the visitors from the provinces crowding the little tables, listen to the new singer while they point out to each other the celebrities who come to Carole's. "Look over there, that's the writer, Maurice Henry, and next to him—who's that?"

"But his young wife, of course, it's she who inspired his latest books, she is Ariane." The singer throws her smile, the smile of a barely tamed panther, toward Maurice, and Maurice scrounges lower in his chair, satisfied, creasing his eyes. What a pleasure it is for him to be known everywhere and admired, to attract every eye, to be liked. Suddenly Cécile feels a great generosity in herself, she feels like a mother giving toys to her child. From her seat, she too smiles to the pretty black singer.

WITH A FLOURISH, Maurice signs his name to the third novel, and puts on her coat, leaving Juliette to him as she goes off to Henriette's. It's become an easy exchange—Juliette as against Henriette. For as to Henriette, he is not to touch her. Henriette is for Cécile alone. The long winter hours close to the glowing fireplace, before Henriette leaves for the theater, with Henriette's head on Cécile shoulder, the vanilla scent of her hair, her low voice signing for Cécile alone, her boyish hand, an energetic, firm hand that knows so well how to make Cécile sigh with happiness—isn't this what she had wanted for so long?

Ever since Henriette has been playing Ariane on the stage, it seems that she too is satisfied with seeing no one but Cécile. Sometimes Cécile becomes worried. Until now, Henriette has never been so faithful. What can be happening to her? Is it because Cécile *is* Ariane that Henriette wants to keep her close, to touch her, to observe her—so long as she playing Ariane? It is a frightful thought that Cécile instantly rejects.

Everything is so complicated in the lives of human beings, that it is better not to ask oneself too many questions; the best thing is to live, to let oneself live; not everybody can begin to go to the depths of things and, like Garry Davis, tear up their passports.

The fact is that since she has Henriette, Cécile is happier, and life with Maurice has become easier.

It is also easier to forgive the wanderings of Maurice since she too has wandered. Returning from an afternoon passed at Henriette's, Cécile smiles almost amiably at a blond head in flight, as she approaches their new apartment. Poor Maurice, she makes excuses for him now; he is so afraid of getting old, the fear of aging devours him. He stands before the mirror for hours, desperately inspecting the wrinkles at the corners of his eyes, or the silvering tint of his hair. How can she resent it if he tries so desperately to prove to himself that he is desirable in spite of his age, that he is still, he is always, the handsome Maurice, over whom all the women are crazy?

How can Cécile be angry at him when presses her in his arms and sighs with so profound an agony, "Cécile, my darling child, how old I am! At your age, you can't understand what it is to get old!"

How can she hold it against him when he takes possession not only of the wives of other men, but of the women she herself has created, signing his name to her books? What does it matter if this gives him pleasure? And since there is Henriette, who is for her alone, what does it matter if she gives Juliette to Maurice so long as she has Henriette? They are even now, they are quits, the balance has been re-established.

TWENTY-THREE YEARS OLD already! Cécile too will begin to believe herself almost an old woman. Just like Maurice, she studies herself in the mirror with anxiety; does the fear of aging take hold of you like a fever?

How far away the Cécile of the past seems to her, the Cécile of Myette's, the seventeen-year-old Cécile with her awakenings at dawn and her solitary walks and her dreams and her love for Mlle Mazoyllet. Her classmates are all married, they all have children, and Cécile stares in the mirror at this boyish body, this sterile body that has not yet produced a single child. It's true that she has such a youthful air, she looks scarcely older than the Cécile of 1944, and yet it seems to her that she is so much changed. She has no child—her only creations are these three literary bastards, which she has not officially recognized, while all Paris whispers more and more that she is their author. Three novels that sell very well, although the serious folk who read Kafka or the existentialist will not stoop to approve this sort of literature—scarcely to be take seriously—where the only subject is love! As though love could be enough of a subject for a serious novel! No, who can take seriously these little novels about Ariane or Juliette, without any theme, without any stylistic effects, and without adherence to any literary school!

Cécile reads the reviews without interest; she always has difficulty in getting herself to realize that it is about books that she has written that people are speaking. Sometimes she becomes saddened. It seems to her that nasty things are being said about some little relative of hers, a sort of cousin whom she may occasionally have visited, who has been a friend, whom she has really been fond of. And then she wants to defend her little relative, to give him the protection of her own name. Hadn't she lived for a number of weeks, for a number of months, with each of these books? With Ariane, Frederic, Anette, Juliette, Sophie, Michel—they are all friends of hers, and now, having departed from her, they must live as they can.

Sometimes in the métro, or on a bench in the street, she sees a young woman or a man sitting and reading a book, and it is *Pas Encore la Jeunesse*, and at times Cécile is tempted to approach and to ask, "Do you like it, madame? Or monsieur? I'm asking you—because I'm the author." And then she realizes how ridiculous that would be. The name of the author is printed on the cover—Maurice Henry. Why then should she interfere?

Of the three books, her favorite nevertheless is the third. It is in this one that Juliette went away, yet at the end of which she found Frederic again—when she admitted the truth to him. But mostly this novel is her favorite because in this book she has portrayed Henriette—a Henriette disguised, and hidden under the name of Claude, and under a mass of blond hair, but nevertheless it is Henriette, so true, such a liar, so untamed. Henriette who knew how to enchant Cécile, how to invade the famished sense of Cécile . . . There is among those pages, between those lines, a lament that must be divined, an emotion that one must perhaps have felt in order to understand the crying truth of it, all naked and wounded. Yes, this volume she has written with the naïve sincerity of the very young whose total innocence alone explains how they can ingenuously avow that which more knowing people would never dare to say.

TO LIVE WITH Maurice when one cannot live without him—this is a very heavy task, and yet Cécile tries by every possible means to establish some order and balance in her life, to bring together all the scattered little pieces of the puzzle that makes up this life, to keep an image of herself—indeed, to preserve her own being. She is too proud ever to show Maurice her heart, preferring to laugh with him, accepting the role of a "twin," taking refuge at Henriette's to forget, and overwhelming her with that overabundance of love which after all has to be deposited somewhere, upon someone, if it is not gathered in where it belongs.

"You, you are a great lover, my darling Cécile," Henriette tells her.

Cécile presses Henriette in her arms, she places her cheek against Henriette's hair, she "tastes" Henriette as she tasted the flowers in her garden, in days gone by, Henriette, with the vanilla-fragrant hair . . .

She would be perfectly happy with Henriette if only Maurice weren't continually present between them. He is present because it is he who arranges their rendezvous, who poses so many curious questions when Cécile returns from Henriette's, who even turns aside the sighing males who would like to approach Henriette after the theater. He who finally manages things so well that Cécile comes to the point of asking herself whether she is really in love with Henriette or whether she sees her, in the last analysis, only because she is still playing her old game for Maurice.

Holding Henriette in her arms, listening to her laugh and chatter of a thousand nothings, Cécile is nevertheless thinking of Maurice. "You are a great lover," Henriette tells her. It is true that Cécile cannot live except in a climate of love.

To love is as indispensable to her as to breathe. But is she really in love with Henriette? Or has Maurice simply succeeded in incorporating Henriette too into his publicity machine?

Sometimes she finds herself composing a discourse that she will make to Maurice, to explain things to him, to ask the meaning from him.

But what can she say to Maurice that will not at the same time admit that she has been wounded? This Maurice to whom Cécile still, after five years of marriage, wants to prove that she is equal to everything, that he has married a woman who knows all and is as sophisticated as any Parisienne. Before Myette, too, Cécile had never been able to let it be seen that she could suffer, or be weak, or that she might be unable to be what Myette wanted her to be: the most amusing, the most intelligent, the most courageous of the girls in the village, the pride of Myette, a girl so completely superior to all the other girls of her age—that which Myette herself, despite all the modesty, would have wanted to be if she could have lived another life.

At all costs, Cécile had, then to let Myette keep the image that she had formed, and in the same way she must now let Maurice keep the image that he has made.

So Cécile goes to the rendezvous that have been arranged by Maurice, thinking of him while she talks with Henriette, talking of Henriette to Maurice when she comes home, and sometimes she begins to detest herself.

Often when Maurice knows Cécile to be in the company of Henriette for an hour at a fashionable bar behind the Champs Elysées, he will suddenly appear, smiling, cane in hand, a flower in his buttonhole. He kisses Henriette's hand, seats himself between the two young women, and Cécile notices how, while his lids are dropped with a feigned indifference, his eyes sparkle with pleasure because there is whispering at the tables all around them.

Henriette doesn't seem to notice anything. She drinks her martini and sucks on an olive, laughs very loud, and under the table she places her boyish hand on Cécile's knee.

If only Maurice wouldn't appear like that, so unexpectedly, if he didn't mix in when she was with Henriette, if he satisfied himself with her Ariane, as in their unspoken agreement, then everything would be in order . . .

But this way Cécile feels herself enmeshed, she no longer knows who she is, nor is she even sure of her own feelings.

She must absolutely separate Henriette from Maurice, take her away from Maurice, so as to know her and to know herself.

IT IS ALWAYS easy for Cécile to wake early in the morning, even at dawn. Up so early, she feels herself ready for life, curious about the day to come, and strong enough to confront whatever there may be before her.

It is the evenings that are difficult for her, the moments that precede sleep. Long ago in the time of her childhood, her father would kiss her when she went up to bed. Then, in the time of Myette, it was her godmama who came into the room and seated herself on the edge of the bed.

"Tell me what happened to you today," she would say. It was the hour of confidences for Cécile, and of memories for Myette. Sleep came little by little, together with a last kiss, while that hand, deformed by labors in the garden, seemed like a bird about to fly about over the covers, alighting here and there to pull up a sheet, to tuck in a blanket.

How peaceably sleep stretched over her then, weaving its veil of dreams.

TODAY IT IS at this same hour that Cécile feels her defeat particularly strongly, now while Maurice turns his heavy body on the bed, which groans beneath him, and while he puts out the light, and the silence established itself, a total silence, in the bedroom.

This end of the day, more and more often without a kiss or a word, leaves her stretched in the night, stiff and straight on her back, her eyes wide open, awaiting the sleep that does not come, while her throat is tight with agony.

What has she done, then? What fault has she committed? She had thought, indeed, that she was doing all that he wanted, being shocking as he wanted, writing as he wanted, amusing him as he wished. She had become famous as the amusing Mme Henry, and yet Maurice seems to be turning away from her.

It is at this hour too that she reviews her day, moment by moment: her work in the morning, still a sort of prisoner of Maurice's, bent with fear and with application over the pages that her pen blackens; her afternoon with Henriette, or at some worldly cocktail party as the companion of the "author of Arianes"; the evenings at the paper or in a café, at the première of a play, or at a concert.

What a waste of time, since the things she writes don't interest her, and the people she meets bore her, and the hours that belong to Maurice are given over to a comedy in which her role is more and more tiresome for her.

And meanwhile, now, Henriette refuses to go out in a threesome, or to dress like Cécile. "I have had enough!" she has declared.

"Good," says Maurice, "I'll find a replacement."

Cécile has no doubt of it. But hasn't she always permitted Maurice everything? She can scarcely begin to protest now.

And so, little by little, there are starlets, dancers, mannequins, each in turn going with Maurice and Cécile on the rounds of cocktail parties—there are blondes and brunettes and redheads, there are sad girls and gay girls. Does Maurice sleep with all of them? He brags a great deal about it, in any case.

Now, their way is set, and Maurice never "deceives" Cécile, since she is kept aware of everything, at one and the same time a participant, an accomplice, and a confidante—and so proud of herself, too, believing herself so adult, so womanly, so modern.

At this price, she can also keep Henriette for herself, without exposing her. Maurice seems at least to have lost interest in Henriette, entirely occupied as he is in finding and training the replacements.

Cécile encounters them everywhere, in the salon, in the bedroom, at all the receptions; she smiles to them politely, gives them back their hairpins, the lipsticks that they have forgotten on her vanity table—poor little girls, they must have a hard life; Cécile knows what it is to love Maurice.

"LORD, HOW HOT it is!" Cécile had forgotten that Paris could be so hot in August. A Paris that becomes emptier every day.

Henriette too must leave the day after tomorrow, for Deauville, to sing in the Casino.

Cécile tries to work, but today the words don't come.

She scratches things out, tears things up, and becomes exasperated over the wrinkled pages.

And at once, the old fear invades her, each time when even for a few hours the phrases hide themselves, the words flee, and ideas evaporate. "Is it the sickness? Has it reached me too?"

The sickness of her father, the sickness of her husband—the impossibility of writing? This fear is always present in her, like the fear that haunts the wives and children of tuberculars.

No, decidedly, she can't write today. Let it go. She'll take a day of vacation.

Cécile gets up.

Maurice is writing letters in his study.

"I'm going for a walk. It's too hot, I can't get anything done. A day of vacation will give me some fresh ideas," she adds, to get him to forgive her laziness.

"Good," says Maurice, for once agreeable. "Why don't you go say goodbye to Henriette?"

"Oh, no!" says Cécile. "I've already said goodbye to her. She's packing her bags and she hates to be bothered then."

"Alright, then go to the Bois de Boulogne, rent a boat, take a ride. Here—here's a thousand francs, amuse yourself."

What generosity! A thousand francs! Cécile descends the stairs at a run. Probably Maurice is expecting one of his recruits, and prefers to remain alone in the house.

But what is there to do the whole day in Paris? Cécile wanders among the almost empty August streets, under the burning sun. She crosses the Seine, lunches in a little bistro along the quay; no, the idea of the Bois de Boulogne says nothing to her, decidedly.

After all, perhaps it is a good idea to go and say goodbye again to Henriette—she won't be seeing her for two weeks. She might even help her pack her bags. Since the play is no longer on, and while Henriette waits for the new play to be adapted from the third novel, in which she will play the part of Juliette or of Claude, Henriette seems less ready to spend her days with Cécile. She no longer has to be Ariane, she no longer needs a model for her role.

Cécile senses this, and suffers from it, but as always it is easier to repress the thought than to express the pain.

Will Henriette be happy, or irritated, then to see her this afternoon? "I'll go," she tells herself. "I'll know soon enough."

AND HERE SHE is in front of Henriette's house, beneath the window of Henriette's room. She raises her head; the sun makes her squint her eyes. Is there a shadow behind the curtain veiling the window? A shadow—two shadows that have approached each other for an instant, and then separated, their movement somehow catching a corner of the thin net curtain, which has trembled.

Henriette's shadow Cécile has recognized at once, a slender shadow, moving lightly; she divines the long scattered hair, and the lithe arm that has made a rounded gesture toward the interior of the room. But it is the other shadow, crossing the curtain, that makes her close her eyes as though she had received a blow.

How well she knows that shadow. How many times hasn't she seen that enormous shadow on the wall of her own bedroom? She opens her eyes again and breathes very deeply, like a drowning person remounting to the surface.

It can only be Maurice. It would have been impossible that Maurice should refrain from appropriating Henriette, and it would have been astonishing if Henriette had not wanted to taste of Maurice. Neither of them has ever said no to a single desire in their lives—why should they have said no, this time? And when Cécile has repeated to them so many times that she is not jealous, that Maurice is free.

Suddenly she recalls the way in which Maurice handed her that thousand franc note and insisted on her passing her day in the Bois de Boulogne, and then she recalls all sorts of details that now seem so evident—the telephone sounding a number of times at the house, and when she had picked it up and said hello there had been a click on the other end. She thought then that it was one of Maurice's mistresses, without even asking herself which. And also Maurice's disinterest toward Henriette in these last months—he who, before, talked of her incessantly, posing all sorts of questions, arranging their meetings. Nailed to the pavement, Cécile looks again at the window facing her. But what proof has she? That shadow that she saw for a second behind the curtain—it could be some other man. Why had her heart begun to thump so? What was the immediate certainty that made her legs wilt as thought they were made of cotton?

And if it was really he—what then? In the long list of his mistresses, Henriette would only be one more. "But Henriette was for me," she keeps thinking—already in the past tense. "I gave him Ariane, I did everything he wanted, all I wanted was to keep Henriette . . ."

Why? Because Henriette was the past, the war, her arrival in Paris, the young girl in uniform, all the mystery, the spirit of adventure, the magic that Paris and Maurice represented in her life, in those days—because Henriette from the beginning had brought her both death and love.

The conquest of Henriette had been the conquest of her fear, it had been a way to establish her equality.

But suppose it is not Maurice? The whole thing is ridiculous! She is making up an entire novel. It's three in the afternoon and Henriette is probably talking to some journalist or other . . .

There is only one way to know, and that is to take out of her purse the door key that Henriette gave her one day when Cécile was to come and wait for her; Cécile has never given back the key.

Cécile has taken the key from her bag, she has gone up to the house and opened the street door, she has begun to mount the stairs, which seem endless to her. And the entire house seems too silent.

This is a terrible thing she is doing. Henriette will never forgive her—nor Maurice either, if it is he. One does not take people by surprise like this. People are free, and one cannot take their love by force.

But she has to know, she has to be sure. Her entire life depends on it. She has come to the day when she can no longer accept the lie, any lie; it is better to have the truth even if it destroys everything. And in her third novel, Juliette had surprised Frederic, just like this—

But it's impossible. Things can't happen entirely in reverse like this. She can't be playing a part taken from her own book, something that she had imagined a year ago.

Here, on the first floor, is Henriette's bedroom, the room Cécile knows so well . . .

Cécile heartbeat reverberates in her ears, her knees tremble, her hand advances hesitantly toward the doorknob. And then she hears Maurice's laughter, that laughter as enormous as his body itself. Behind the closed door—from the bed, surely—Maurice is laughing like that, as though he were laughing at Cécile. Once before, in the first year of their marriage, Cécile had entered a room and found Maurice with a woman. She had then sworn to herself that she would never do it again. And yet it seems that everything is beginning all over again and the she is there once more, that the same scene must unroll as in a film one has seen before. But this time the woman is Henriette.

Behind the closed door there is shuffling noise, as of a pillow falling to the floor, and then a sigh, a throaty growl . . .

Cécile reddens violently, as though she had been caught peeking through the keyhole, or in the midst of opening a letter addressed to someone else.

No, there isn't even any need for her to go in. She deposits the key on the floor just in front of the door, and softly she descends the stairway, she goes out into the street, into the pale light of an indifferent sun . . .

She had let Ariane be taken from her and now she has let Henriette be taken, too.

THE KEY DEPOSITED before the door is found by Henriette when she leaves her room with Maurice.

"What's this? What's this key doing her?" she says as she picks it up. "I must have let it drop a while ago." There is a bit of red ribbon tied to the key, and Henriette knits her brows. "It's my extra key," she says. "I loaned it to someone. Who was it then?"

She looks at Maurice, become pale, and then red.

"It was Cécile who had this key," she cries. "Maurice, I'm sure of it, she hadn't given it back to me—she must have come here."

"What of it?" says Maurice. "You know perfectly well Cécile is broad minded, and even if it was she, you can see she didn't make anything of it. Too bad, though, if it was she, that she didn't come in. I wouldn't have minded having the two of you together—" and he laughs his laugh of a goodhearted child.

"You think Cécile would have wanted to?" asks Henriette.

"Why not?" says Maurice. "What harm would it be? I even think it's time that she tried something new. It could be useful for our next book, too." When Maurice speaks of Cécile's books to Henriette he always says "our." "You ought to suggest it to her," he adds. And he bends over and kisses Henriette's hand, so much the man of the world, so much at his ease, so much a part of the twentieth century, that Henriette too smiles and says, "Yes, why not?"

ONCE AGAIN, CÉCILE has made no trouble.

She has simply forgotten Henriette—totally. She has a power of forgetfulness like no one else. She can completely eject someone who has deceived her from her consciousness, from her heart, from her body, as though rubbing them out with an eraser.

If she could only reject Maurice in this way. But with Maurice, she cannot do it. To reject Henriette is almost easy, but to reject Maurice would be to kill—at once and the same time—her father, her childhood, her dreams, her first love, all her life . . .

It is easier to kill Cécile than to kill Maurice.

And so Cécile has set herself to kill Cécile . . .

HE WAS CERTAIN that Cécile and Henriette would encounter each other, "afterward." They move in the same circles, half-artistic, half-socialite. Henriette is the first to catch sigh of Cécile, at a vernissage, and she waits, to know how to react. Cécile tells herself, She no longer exists, and raises her champagne glass to her, smiling politely. She doesn't advance toward Henriette, neither to accuse her nor to forgive her, and Maurice, repeating pleasantries to the two famous actresses whom he holds lightly on either arm, speeds a rapid glance to the left toward Henriette, and to the right toward Cécile, like a general stock of a battleground.

But there is no battle.

Cécile turns back toward a most elegant young man who is discussing Kafka, to whom he modestly compares himself. At this moment, the young man has a profound admiration for Cécile, for she listens without taking her eyes from him. The young man admires all those who listen attentively to him; he fails to realize that Cécile doesn't hear a single word he utters. The young man writes poems, and speaks about them a great deal. He likes to describe his labors and his inspiration and the various reactions of his readers. Before the arrival of Henriette, Cécile, trapped by the young poet, had been astonished to hear him taking himself so seriously. The idea would never have come to her to extend herself over her own "literary labors"—this labor is something that she does because she has to, because Maurice has ordered her to, and that she tries to do as well as she can, with the patient application of a conscientious student, searching for the exact word, the precise image. But from that—to speak about it, to describe the state of her soul, to note the reactions of her readers, that would be absurd. Even if her anonymity no longer existed, Cécile would be unable to speak of what she wrote any more than would she extend herself to describe in detail her efforts at gardening in Myette's yard, dilating on the scent of the blossoms and of the earth, and the effect produced by the completed flower beds.

Now she no longer listens; her eyes have turned to a gray blue, for she is no longer amused. These are her eyes when pensive. The young poet watches himself reflected in them, while he goes on reciting the names of each Parisian personality who has written to felicitate him.

Cécile thinks: I have lost her, and I don't want to remind myself of her anymore. Nothing remains of her except a character in a novel. There is no more Henriette. There will never again be anymore Henriette. Only a Claude, blond, between the pages of a book. That is the flow of life, the birth and the death, of plants, of men, of loves. Now it still gives me pain to look at her there, in front of that abstract painting that harmonizes with the color of her hair. It still gives me pain, but this pain, too, will disappear, little by little, if I don't think about her—

"Excuse me," Cécile says to the young man, and she moves off. There is a friend of Maurice's, whom she has seen from a distance, and who has smiled to her. Cécile catches the smile, approaches. Around her there is this brouhaha of voices. Maurice's friend bends over her hand. Everyone is most elegant and well-bred and everyone plays on in the game of life . . .

IN THESE YEARS following on 1950, Paris is free, Paris is rich, life has become so amusing in Paris. The war is very far away, with its rationing, its failures of electricity, its bombardments, its restrictions . . .

This is the period of the cellar clubs of St. Germain-des-Prés, of beatniks and of Brigitte Bardot, of Dior's New Look and "St. Trop," and of rock 'n' roll. Those who have the money can go skiing in Switzerland in the winter and waterskiing on "the coast" in summer; in a few hours one is in New York, and Françoise Sagan and television and the cinema create wave after wave of the New Wave.

Cécile has stopped seeing Henriette, but she lets herself be seen with actresses, models, altogether like Maurice. All at once life has gone to her head, like wine. She no longer knows who she is, and she arranges things so that there will be enough noise in her life to keep her from hearing the slightest complaint from within herself.

Maurice's mistresses are all friends of hers, she discusses them with Maurice, consoles them when he leaves them, distracts them when he wants a bit of peace so as to approach a newer conquest. This is what is known as a modern marriage, and if anyone were to ask Cécile, "Are you happy?" she would still immediately reply, "Of course."

Yet every day she withdraws to her room—not to the study that Maurice has installed for her, but to her own room in the hours of Maurice's absence, and on her big bed she writes for herself—without revealing a word of this to anyone.

In any case it is not the sort of story he would like. It is too romantic, it has too much description, too much emotion. It is the story of a little girl who lives in the country. A solitary little girl, a dreamer; nothing really happens to her—there are only her dreams. No, such a subject wouldn't be attractive to Maurice.

It gives her a strange pleasure to write like this, a stolen pleasure, an illicit pleasure—it is a sort of infidelity.

Cécile hides herself away with her little heroine, her Veronica, in a far more total way than she could do with Henriette.

She hurries to shut herself in with Veronica, her heart trembling, as though she were shutting herself in to make love with a real young girl.

It is a strange liaison, for isn't Veronica what Cécile herself had been at one time? Bent over the paper, she closes her eyes again to see that little girl with her long hair, devouring her books, her apron pocket filled with figs, perched in a tree, or swimming naked in the river, dreaming about life, about love, trying to forget all hatred, and the war, separations, and the adult world that tramples everything around her, destroying childhood and killing dreams.

Would this little girl have been able to build her life as a woman on some other basis?

It is in describing Veronica that Cécile sets herself to thinking about Cécile. Perhaps it's my own fault, she tells herself now for the first time. Perhaps he who asks nothing, receives nothing. And what has she asked of Maurice, up until this very day? Nothing, ever—except his presence. It has always seemed to me so marvelous and generous of him to have been so good as to want a little peasant like me. How could I in addition be so audacious as to ask him for his total love! And now, isn't it too late? Too late because he has become altogether meaningless to me?

TOO LATE TO begin all over, then, but not too late to keep on.

She is in a taxi with Maurice. It's night, but the heat is suffocating. Yesterday they were in Paris, and the rain fell in torrents, it was cold, it was winter.

Now they are in North Africa, just for three days.

This is what life is like with Maurice; Paris, London, Brussels, Madrid—Maurice jumps into a plane the way anyone else jumps onto a bus. This time, only a few days ago, he said, "You want to come? A bit of local color will be good for you—you can use it in your next book. I have to spend three days in Algeria and Casablanca—some rights on a book to buy—it's written by an Arab."

They have taken the author home. It's midnight, the taxi, in all this heat, suddenly enters a lane of palms.

"You know," says Maurice, "there are still some brothels around here, though officially they're all supposed to be closed up, I think. But if it would amuse you, I can ask the driver. If there's a girl you like, you can choose her for yourself."

To go into a brothel, like a man, to have a man's experience, to show Maurice that she wouldn't hesitate, that nothing shocks her anymore . . . and besides, her natural curiosity is still with her. To know everything, to taste everything—isn't that the only way one can write about everything?

"Yes, I'd like it," she says.

Maurice smiles. "I knew you'd like it all right," he says.

Ah, how well she has convinced him of her personality.

"It's here," says the chauffeur.

They are in front of a house surrounded by high walls, over-reached by blossoming trees and with climbing vines covering the stones. The driver speaks through a peep-hole and the door opens. A woman ushers them in. All is so calm and so natural, the garden is so beautiful, the sky over their heads is filled with stars.

A bordel—Cécile had imagined a sordid kind of place, and not this quietude, these flowers, this nighttime heat, this bare-footed woman walking before them, rolling her hips.

They enter the house. The woman opens a door and Cécile finds herself in a rather large, square room, stone-floored, and well lighted. The room is empty, unfurnished except for a table in the middle, with a smiling woman sitting behind it, like a schoolmistress. And all around the room, on benches against the calcimined walls, there sit young women, about twenty of them, some smiling, others serious, some so young that one would believe they are still children. A number are wearing Arab clothes, and others are in short dresses.

There are white women, and there are little Tonkinese faces, and black women with long necks and short hair, and there are half-castes. No one seems surprised to see a man in continental Parisian attire, with a young woman at his side; the madam seated behind the table stretches out her hand toward the girls and asks Maurice to choose as though he were about to hand out a school prize.

"Which do you want?" Maurice asks. And the other Cécile at once appears, the shadow, the one who watches, and who observes Cécile, she looks at the room, she breathes in the odor, she listens to the sounds. It is no longer Cécile who is there, Cécile disappears like a cloud of smoke; the shadow remains, the shadow notes each detail of this adventure, the shadow tells her, You are one of those rare women who has been able to enter a bordel and do something that is reserved for men only, you have the right to experience everything. You are writing books so you must know more than other women. Here, take this little Tonkinese, the one with a face like a golden apple—the apple of the tree of knowledge of good and evil.

The little Tonkinese, or Siamese, or Chinese, wears white silken trousers and a black blouse with a standing collar. She is so small, she is shorter than Cécile. She looks to be fifteen or at most sixteen. What is she doing here? How did she get all the way here, so young and so far from home?

Watching Cécile solemnly with her slanted eyes, the girl smiles to Maurice, and follows them with docility, like a little Siamese cat.

On the first floor there are rooms, they are clean, the bed is made. The three of them stand looking at each other. Someone knocks and the door opens, a small Arab boy, scarcely nine years old, enters, carrying a tray with a bottle and three glasses. He greets them gravely, disposes his tray without saying a word, and withdraws. What is he thinking? Does he think at all?

The little Asiatic doesn't speak French, not a single word—she approaches the bed, undoes the pins of her chignon, and her long hair unrolls.

THE STORY OF Veronica writes itself slowly, between voyages, parties, receptions. There is rain in Copenhagen, it snows in New York, and Rome in summer is suffocatingly hot.

Photographs of Cécile Henry and her famous husband often

appear in the press. "M. and Mme Maurice Henry at the pre-mière at the Vieux Colombier . . . M. and Mme Maurice Henry with Marilyn Monroe in New York . . ."

In Rome, Henriette, who is singing in a nightclub, comes to say hello to them. She has an Italian lover, she has changed, she is less untamed, more polished, her hair is shorter, less black, the songs she sings are more commercial. She wears gowns from the leading couturiers. This is no longer the Henriette of nearly ten years ago, fierce, rebellious, the girl with the hoarse voice singing the verses of Apollinaire.

In New York, Eddie appears at their hotel to say hello to them, and Cécile goes for a walk with him on Fifth Avenue, facing the park, but while they walk side by side she doesn't take his arm as she would have done in Paris, this would be awkward for both of them in New York. They talk of everything and nothing, and of Henriette and of Eddie's work.

Eddie says, "These books signed by Maurice Henry—it's you who wrote them, Cécile—isn't it true, what everyone says?"

"I collaborated a little," says Cécile.

New York is a strange city to which she can never habituate herself. It is a nervous, inhuman city, an artificial city made for machines, not for humans. But Maurice finds himself at ease there at once. At bottom he is an American by instinct if not by nationality. Sitting at a bar, a Manhattan in hand, between a film agent and a producer, discussing ideas for films, author's rights, available actors, Maurice, despite his French accent, seems exactly like the two other men, he speaks like them, thinks like them.

A modest red ribbon of the Legion of Honor on his lapel makes a good impression. He offers cigars and he gets Paris on the telephone. The producer smiles to Cécile, who comes in with Eddie. "Your wife looks so French, so charming," the producer exclaims, "a real French girl."

Cécile climbs onto a stool; she too smiles and orders a drink and lights a cigarette. It seems to her that she has learned all the motions, like a dog trained for the circus.

"Does your wife write too?" asks the agent, who has perhaps heard some rumors circulating.

"My wife is talented mostly for the theater," says Maurice. "She dances and sings very well, but she won't hear of developing and using her talents."

"What a pity," says the producer. He looks at Eddie and Cécile, and he asks himself whether he could arrange a date with her. He had lunched, yesterday, with Maurice and a model; he knows that Maurice has a rendezvous in an hour with a little out-of-work actress; if the husband is so free, this young Frenchwoman who exhibits herself out walking with Negroes must also have very free ideas.

He likes her; she talks very little, she has the virtuous look of the sort of young women who hid their desires behind angelic faces and polite manners, and besides, he has never yet slept with a Frenchwoman.

"BUT IT'S VERY good, this little story," says Maurice, back in Paris, as Cécile finds him before her desk holding "Veronica" in his hands. "Why have you never said anything to me about it? You little squirrel! It's charming, original—it must be published."

And Cécile is still melting with pleasure under the compliment coming from Maurice. "But first," he goes on, "we'll have to stretch this out a little. It's too short, it has to be made into a novel. Can't you add a part—after Veronica's marriage? Wait—we'll have to make her unfaithful, that little one. Yes, I have an idea!"

He sits down before her desk and, as always, repeats, "I ask myself what you would write without me. It would be unpublishable."

To change Veronica according to his wishes? Cécile feels herself beaten in advance. Her fear of making any opposition to Maurice seizes her again—the fear losing him if she offers him any opposition. And yet something has changed her. She takes refuge in silence, she doesn't reply to Maurice, doesn't argue with him. She has learned so many things, in writing Veronica.

Perhaps she has found new forces? No, she will not give way this time, she will not give him Veronica as she gave him Ariane and Henriette, and the whole of her life.

PERHAPS WHAT SHE must do is to flee. To flee? What does one do, to flee? Juliette was able to flee, but Cécile is not Juliette, and where should she go and how should she live? And then there is always her worry about Myette. Always this inability to return to her side and to admit that she has been beaten by life.

If Cécile occasionally voices some protestation, Maurice remarks, "After all, you are perfectly free." But she is not free, she is a slave, and Maurice knows it.

She thinks, then, about trying to flee, but she remains. Her escape is sublimated in her writing. It is Juliette who goes away. To describe Juliette's courage, her independence, the details of her departure from home, helps Cécile to stay. It seems so useless to flee when she doesn't know where to go. Cécile is of the race of women who do not leave their man, unless they love another. The only reason to break with Maurice, the only valid reason, would have been if she were in love elsewhere. But to leave toward a great emptiness . . . She has friends, but no lovers. And even in these friendships, she does not totally give herself; rather, she lets herself be loved, happy that someone is tender to her, attentive, worried about her health, her mood, happy to laugh with her without afterthought, without any intrigue.

Friendships of this sort she finds all about her, in abundance. Young actors whom Maurice has taken under his wing, young journalists, painters, boys and girls, past and present mistresses—Cécile passes many alight afternoon with them. A large number of the boys are homosexuals, and Cécile listens to their tales; a large number of the girls are promiscuous and unhappy, and Cécile consoles them as best she can.

What pains her is that she doesn't succeed in attaching herself to anyone. She studies them as always, imprinting in herself their features, their voices, their adventures with a clinical detachment. Just as when Maurice repeats to her, "Take notes."

She doesn't take notes in a notebook but within herself. She is only unhappy at not being able to love anymore, as she had loved Myette, and Mademoiselle—with purity. As she loved Henriette, with sensuality, as she loved Maurice, with passion.

As she "loved" Maurice—but doesn't she still love him? Cécile asks herself this, now, every day.

The feeling she has for him, on the nights when he is there, the nights when he still takes her in his arms—is it love? Or is it still sexual curiosity, is it still sexual attachment? And yet while Maurice sleeps, encircling Cécile's light body with his arms, when she makes herself a place against him, like a cat turning around and around on the sofa until it has dug exactly the nest that fits its body, Cécile at last for some moments has the feeling that Maurice is a kind of hollowed mold into which her shoulders, her torso, her legs come to fit themselves, exactly into their place. There is no need for words nor for excuses, nor for explanations. All is there between them in those short moments. Cécile sighs, then, in relief. Maurice tightens his clasp, and Cécile's cheek, resting against Maurice's chest, feels the beating of that mysterious heart. She forgives him everything then, she cannot imagine that she could leave him, and one day love another man.

Is it really possible that this should suffice for a woman, that these few stolen moments of happiness are enough? That they can weigh down the balance when the other side is filled with misery, fear, hunger, and abandonment?

Perhaps it is enough for the woman who lives her various womanly lives in the books she writes. If Cécile found herself unsatisfied, Ariane, in counterbalance, was happy. Juliette succeeded in escaping. Frederic bends over her with solicitude and love. And Veronica has recovered the purity of her childhood.

It is therefore easier to surrender Cécile than to surrender Veronica. It is on the subject of Veronica that Maurice becomes angry, thundering, and smashing his clenched fist against his desk. He wants changes in the little novel that Cécile has written for herself, in hiding, and Cécile, with her habitual submissiveness, has already agreed on principle to a revision. But

Maurice wants things in it that she doesn't want. More scandal, more scabrous incidents, and the introduction of a character resembling himself, that he has for a long time been suggesting to Cécile, and that is somehow a pleasing notion to Maurice—a character who speaks like him, and in whom he will at last see himself live. Cécile uses such weapons as she possesses—her own peculiar weapons. She delays, she suggests going away for a few days, writing in the country where her inspiration, she says, will come more easily; she hopes that Maurice will get tired and forget Veronica.

"I'VE HAD ENOUGH!" shouts Maurice one morning. "Do you want to ruin this book? Is that what you want? You have the material for a perfect novel, that would sell very well, something original, interesting, and instead of writing it the way I tell you to, you obstinately persist in sabotaging it. But don't you understand at all that without me, without my help, you are simply incapable of writing a book by yourself? It would never be published, it would never sell, and instead of listening to what I tell you, you get obstinate! I have never seen such a mule-head! I want this to be written this coming week, and written the way I tell you to! Is that understood?"

"No!" cries Cécile, beside herself and astonished at her own courage.

"No?" repeats Maurice, as astonished by this sudden courage as Cécile herself. "No?" he repeats again. "You prefer to have me work myself to death, and that we shouldn't have a sou—rather than to listen to my suggestions?"

Slowly, without taking his eyes from her, from the hypnotized eyes of Cécile, he undoes the buckle of his belt, he pulls out the belt, which slips around his body and hangs limply at the end of his hand.

"Are you going to force me to beat you?" he asks.

He won't dare, thinks Cécile, he cannot dare to do such a thing. But when she says "no" a second time, it is not because she thinks he will not dare, it is perhaps because she hopes he will dare. For doesn't she know that it is necessary for the drama to explode so that she may be freed, that Maurice has yet to beat and wound her, much more seriously than he has done until now?

Without any difficulty, Maurice has seized hold of Cécile's wrists, which he presses behind her back, while he throws her on the bed. His belt comes down on the doubled, twisting body. After each stroke of the belt, he repeats, "Well, are you going to obey, or not?"

It is only when Cécile senses that she is now strengthened enough by hatred that she replies—defeated for Veronica, but the victor for Cécile—"yes."

IT SEEMS TO her that she has been sick for years, sick with fear—fear of not being equal to things, fear of seeming inexperienced, fear of displeasing, fear of saying "no"—and then, she has once more said "yes," but this time, the "yes" has been the stroke of the scissors that has begun to cut through the cords that hold her prisoner. She has said "yes," she has given up Veronica too, but she has ceased to feel, she has entirely ceased to feel even her fear. She has therefore also been freed of fear.

And yet there still remains so much weakness in her. The idea of leaving, of quitting Maurice, is still something that seems to her impossible. For Maurice is a drug, and it is just as difficult to leave him as it is to leave an addiction to a drug.

As for him, he is in good humor. *Veronica*, having become a novel, does well from the start. It has already been sold to a film producer. There is talk about Brigitte Bardot for the leading role. There is talk of Pierre Brasseur or of Orson Welles for the part of the husband.

Returning from a business luncheon, Maurice is filled with projects and zest. "Cécile," he cries in his thundering voice, from the doorway, "Cécile, I have a proposition for you. That South American countess we met last week is giving a reception and she wants you to sing there."

"Wants me to sing?" repeats Cécile. "Is she crazy?"

"Why not?" says Maurice. "I told her that you sing, dance, do wonderful imitations; she finds you ravishing, I even think she has a thing for you. One of her friends, a young pianist, is going to play, I am going to do some magic tricks, and you will sing. That will liven up the reception and who knows, it may open a new career for you—you ought to do something of your own."

"Good God!" thinks Cécile, almost laughing. As though she did nothing! Her fourth novel has just been published. But of course, all this doesn't count for Maurice, these are his books, and in his eyes Cécile does nothing but collaborate on them in the vaguest way. "Yes," continues Maurice, "I even ask myself whether you wouldn't do better before an audience than before a blank sheet of paper. You remember, years ago I suggested you should go into films."

AT THE COUNTESS'S reception, then, Cécile sings, accompanying herself on a guitar, and she has great success.

The reception, given in a private villa on the Avenue du Bois, is a brilliant affair—all Paris is there. Maurice loves this type of distraction. He mingles in the crowd of pretty women who flock around him; he plays his eternal role of Don Juan, bringing a glass of champagne to one, fetching a silken scarf, a fan to another.

And Cécile discovers that it is so much more agreeable to play-act from a distance, protected by greasepaint and a costume, than to mix with the crowd. This first time, she has stage fright, but nevertheless she savors the laughter behind the improvised screens, the camraderie with a homosexual young pianist, and with a young woman who is to follow her with a dance number.

The young dancer has long black hair, and for a moment Cécile regrets having years ago cut her own hair short. The dancer has such a white skin—the skin of Henriette—but she doesn't have the scent of Henriette. Cécile raises the girl's hair, weighing it in her palms; she passes her hand over the warm nape of the young dancer. Cécile smiles, but she reflects that never again will any woman, even the most beautiful, be able to hurt her as Henriette hurt her; she will never again permit herself to be hurt, or to love—since the two go together.

The public applauds, the elegant crowd of tout-Paris, the head bending under the big hats, the fans palpitating, the men smiling as they whisper, "It's Cécile, people say she is the real author of *Pas Encore la Jeunesse* and all those other books of Maurice Henry. The scandalous wife of the scandalous Maurice. Yes, look at her in that costume—what pretty legs. People say she doesn't care for men, didn't you know? Just look at the way Lili Dumont stares at her—that's the little dancer who's next. Oh, Lili won't be wasting her time with Cécile Henry!"

Later, Darryl Zanuck appears with Juliette Gréco, Simone Signoret gets into a conversation with Orson Welles, Bernard Buffet is arguing with Aly Khan, and Carmen Tessier is there taking down gossip for her column. It is the tout-Paris of the arts, and the pretty redheaded countess draws Cécile aside in the garden. "You were adorable," she says. "You sing marvelously and your husband tells me that you dance equally well. Why don't you study and become a dancer or singer? With such talents . . ."

Cécile smiles distractedly while watching Lili Dumont, who has gone into the salon, dressed in a very small bikini in cloth of gold, so minute that she is actually almost naked. Her lovely, supple body twists under a spotlight directed upon her; her round, swelling breasts escape from the tiny brassiere, whose straps have slipped.

"I would die of shame if I had to show myself like that, almost naked in public," whispers the countess. "And you, Cécile?"

Cécile doesn't reply. Her eyes attentively follow that body, twisting like a serpent in the greenery, the whole body scintillating. Hasn't she too been showing herself naked in public, for years? During all the years since her marriage?

The blood mounts brightly to her cheeks, the blood of shame. It seems to her that she has shown herself far more nakedly than Lili Dumont, so naked in the skin of Ariane, so naked in the skin of Veronica, so naked in the skin of Juliette. Luckily, readers are far more blind than spectators.

HOW MUCH SIMILARITY there is in playing a person on the stage and in creating one on paper.

In both cases, one must "become" the personage. One must think like the person, see the person inwardly, feel the person, make the person live.

But the theater, to Cécile, seems a better way to escape. She does not believe in herself enough to think that she can live from writing alone.

Maurice has so insistently repeated to her that without him, without his name, nothing she could write would have the slightest interest. Didn't he tell her disdainfully, one day in the country, "The time I have to lose, correcting all this jumble of little stupidities that's so important to you!" This was at the time when she was refusing to change Veronica in the way he wanted.

Maurice no longer hides the fact that Cécile "helps him" write his books. But how he minimizes her part, and how he has managed to persuade her that she is no writer!

Then perhaps the theater, with her singing and dancing, remains as a last life raft for her? And Maurice senses that Cécile is leaving him little by little, he senses it by a thousand signs that Cécile herself isn't aware of. By a blush on her forehead, a change of color in her eyes, by her handwriting which no longer looks the same on her manuscripts, by a new docility, too—a disdainful docility now.

MAURICE HAS RECEIVED the telegram and opened it while Cécile is away from the house. She will be back soon and he will have to tell her. Already once before he had to tell her of the death of her parents and he hadn't been able to do it. Now he must tell her of the death of Myette. He knows how much Cécile loves Myette and how Myette was a second mother for her. He knows too that if Cécile has remained with him until now, this too was largely because of Myette—so that Myette might not know she is unhappy. To show her suffering is impossible for Cécile. Now, Cécile will be free.

IT'S TRUE THAT she will go away, leave him.

He knows it. He holds the telegram in his hand. Presently, he will have to tell her, "She is dead," and after that Cécile will no longer have any reason to remain, to keep quiet, to accept everything.

And yet he loves her—in his own strange manner he loves her and he understands her and even today, after years of marriage, when she comes into a room and he looks at her he feels the same emotion he felt the first time on that station platform, when he saw that little girl dressed up as a woman, with her eyes filled with terror, and her smiling lips. She was brave, already then. But wouldn't she have done better to have admitted at once, "I'm so frightened . . . it hurts . . ." and wouldn't she then have better succeeded in holding him, in keeping him from wounding her?

Isn't it her own fault that their marriage has come to this end? No one has the right to allow himself to be hurt like that by another person.

And now it is too late, too late to hold her, to tell her that they have both been mistaken, that he is not as cruel as she has permitted him to be, and that he might even have been able to be faithful to her if she had dared to ask it.

For he loves this child as he has loved no woman in his life, since that first moment at the station, and if she had known how much he loved her she would have been able to keep him for always.

Of course I can ask her not to go, make an effort to keep her, because then she would stay. But would she stay for love, or for pity? Pity because I am getting old, because I'm alone, because she knows that I can't even write, and I don't want her pity. What I once was for her—the brilliant Parisian who knows everything, who can do anything—that, I am no longer. The image has been destroyed. I am no more than an aging libertine, too fat, with a face already filled with wrinkles, with graying hair . . . while she is twenty-eight, the most gracious age for a woman, the age when they open to full bloom, emerge from their long adolescence, and at last become women . . . Keep her? What for? What can I give her? I am able only to make her suffer.

She is just beginning to live, she is climbing toward the top of the hill while I'm on my way down the other side. We cannot meet again. It is evening. The shadows are descending over Paris, they invade the room, they darken the Seine that flows beneath the windows. Maurice lets himself fall heavily into an armchair.

TOMORROW MORNING.

I'll leave tomorrow morning.

But how is she to tell it to Maurice? How can she tell him, Maurice, this is the last night? In the theater, in novels, there is a scene, the woman leaves, slamming the door, or there is a lover waiting for her in front of the house.

How can one say to this man with whom one has lived for ten years, the first man one has loved, and to whom one has been totally enslaved, "I'm leaving tomorrow morning"? As though one is ending a visit that has lasted too long.

All night long, Cécile, awake, turns the phrases in her head.

The hours pass. Maurice sleeps, his back to her.

Am I really going to leave him? Go away all by myself? Toward what? This man who humiliated me so much, made me suffer so much, and who nevertheless became all that I had.

All night long, Cécile reviews the years that have passed, with the lucidity of a prisoner awaiting execution.

Her arrival in Paris, her discovery of Maurice with the dancer from the Folies Bergère, Myette's visit, her life of solitude, her first emergence with Maurice into the cafés, her desperate efforts to please him, her labor over the Ariane books, her love for Henriette, and her relation to the women scattered through Maurice's life . . . Wherever she went, that fear that she never wanted to admit to herself, of seeing Maurice flirting, seducing, neglecting her completely except when he needed her for a new book, or a new publicity idea.

How could she have been able to live like that? How is it that she has not been annihilated by this life, long before?

On this night, Cécile finally makes her decision. It is her last night.

"Tomorrow morning. I'll leave tomorrow morning."

IT HAS TAKEN ten years.

Ten years to free herself.

How long a time since that day when she sees herself again, running in the lane, leaping over a little wall so as to come more quickly to this man.

It has taken ten years to be able at last to say "no" to him. "No" to his tyranny, "no" to his infidelities, "no" to his daily egotism, and—finally—"no" to his sadism.

In the morning she tells him calmly that she is leaving.

She has flung some things—mostly useless—pell-mell into her valise.

Now she is ready, she has closed the valise, she has lowered a veil over her face.

Maurice doesn't say a word.

It is in a total silence that she looks at him, one more time.

She advances toward the door. The valise is light, she opens the door, she doesn't turn back. Maurice does not budge.

IT WAS SO simple, then—why had she waited ten years? This was all she had had to do—a few simple movements—to open a few drawers, to close a valise, to go down a stairway.

Ten years and one night.

PART 3

Cécile opens her eyes. At dawn her eyes are gray like the dawn, gray as the dew. Presently they will be blue, and later still they will turn yellow, yellow as corncobs dried in the sun.

But there is neither dew here, nor are there any corncobs. There is nothing but a little single apartment, a studio in the rue d'Assas. Cécile is alone in a narrow bed which will later be turned into a divan, and Minou, faithful, but become almost blind with age sleeps rolled into a ball on a pillow at the foot of the bed.

Cécile has brought with her only Minou and an album of photographs of long ago, of the time in Gascony, showing a Cécile with a laughing air, climbing a tree, her braid tangled around her neck; or there is Cécile with her arm around Anette in the courtyard of the school, or there is Cécile seated on the steps of the house, beside Myette.

A photo album, and a leather-bound book—one only—as a symbol. A large book bound in green leather, with a title engraved in letters of gold, and with hundreds of blank white pages inside . . .

It is strange to be so alone and to live so silent a life after ten years of the boisterous life with Maurice.

The silence still at times makes Cécile jump. She hasn't got used to it, nor to no longer hearing the entrance door slam, and the thunderous voice cry out, "Quick, Cécile, quick, I'm in a hurry."

At present, Cécile's life unrolls with perfect precision. It is an austere life. In the morning, up early as in the old days, she prepares her breakfast and then begins her hours of practice, preparing her dance number. Three times a week she goes to the gymnastic lessons, three times a week to her dance lessons. The afternoons are devoted to visits to the agents, to her dressmaker for the repair of costumes that are continuously getting torn, continuously having to be redesigned, and her evenings are devoted to her job.

She had found her job immediately after leaving Maurice, through Henriette, who was just then passing through Paris, stopping only for a short nightclub engagement. The same nightclub was ready to take on a good striptease dancer—but with something new, something original?

Why not?

She had been doing a moral striptease for ten years, why not do one in the flesh? It is less humiliating to show her body than her soul, less humiliating to dance nude, protected by the footlights, by her makeup, by an established role, than to show herself again and again in her nakedness in the parts she played in her life, in welcoming to her house her husband's mistresses, in playing the modern woman playing at indifference, playing at perversion. Displaying her naked breasts, after ten years of marriage with Maurice Henry, is really so much more simple, more honest, and more pure. It is almost a relief.

And besides, how wonderful no longer to have to act a part, but to be the part. She is now something that can easily be defined, a woman of the world, gone bad. A woman writer who has gone bad. A nude dancer, she no longer plays a shocking role, she *is* that shocking being.

A shocking being who lives an almost monastic life.

After her lesson in gymnastics, Cécile takes a shower, has salad for lunch, and then walks all the way to her impresario's office on the Champs Elysées. Walking is excellent for the muscles.

The impresario's office reminds her of the atmosphere around Maurice—the smoke, the cigar smell, the ringing telephones, the continuous agitation.

"Yes, I may have a very good offer for you, if it interests you—a contract for the Folies Bergère, six months, well paid." Six months of regular salary. Cécile jumps at the offer—she will surely accept.

While awaiting the final answer, she walks home, enrapt. She cleans the apartment, prepares dinner for herself and Minou, mends her stockings, rests for half an hour, and then goes off to the nightclub, to do her striptease number.

It has been like this every day for four months. After her number, she removes her makeup, hangs up her things, gets ready to go home, always alone.

The nightclub clients who have tried to make dates with her have been disappointed. The owner, M. Antoine, shakes his head. "Cécile is a real nun," he says. "I haven't ever seen her with anyone, man or woman." And one night, no longer able to endure the mystery, he demands of Cécile, "But really, Cécile tell me the truth, with whom do you make love?" For M. Antoine is unable to accept the idea that a young woman, healthy and pretty, with a body such as Cécile displays to his clients every night, can live without making love. It's impossible.

Cécile begins to laugh, and replies, "It's a secret." She kisses M. Antoine on the cheek and runs off, her little round valise in her hand, her short hair glistening, smooth as a schoolboy's, her face, now that her work is finished, clean of makeup. Light-footed in her ballet slippers, she is as in the fable, *Légère et court vêtue*.

At the house, at home, she goes to sleep in her cold bed, a maiden's narrow cot, with Minou purring at her feet. She falls asleep quickly, her body fatigues and her spirit empty. Sometimes, rarely, on an afternoon when she has no agent to meet, she sits at the table that serves for her meals and as a dressing table, a kitchen work table, and a makeup table, and she tries to write.

SHE HAD PLACED some white sheets before her, taken a pen in hand, and waited. But nothing had come. Nothing.

Yes, Maurice was right, she is not writer, she never was one, she could only write when Maurice was there to help her; by herself, she cannot do it. Even the story of Veronica would have been worthless if he had not revised and corrected it.

On the white sheet of paper she drew a flower, and then a

dream bird. And then she had crumpled up the sheet, rolling it into a ball and throwing it at Minou.

But Minou grown too old, is no longer in the mood to play. Even Minou had no use for her ball of paper.

STILL, SHE HAS received several letters from Maurice, begging her to write something, no matter what—stories, descriptions, articles—that he might make use of.

Paris is surprised that not a single book by Maurice Henry has appeared recently. Several of his "collaborators" had left Maurice, some of his film writers are working elsewhere, and Cécile had become his chief source of literary production.

When Cécile receives Maurice's letters, she hesitates to open them; sometimes she tears them up unopened. What use would it be? She can't write, she is a dancer now. Hasn't Maurice himself always told her that she had more talent for dancing than for writing? Besides, these letters contain nothing but these request for her services. Maurice never asks how she is, or if she is in need of anything, he never asks her to come back. He let her go, and he never asks her to come back.

So it is; she has failed in her life, failed in her marriage, failed in love or in what she had taken for love.

Yes, since that day she had run breathless toward Maurice, believing he was about to leave, she had imprinted a single seal of their union; Maurice was the dispenser of her pleasure. She had taken that pleasure for love, since love is a gift, but what had she given to Maurice? Her youth, her curiosity, yes, but where these things gifts? What she had given him, any other young girl could have given him just as well. She had given him nothing and she had asked nothing of him.

The New Testament that she had read in childhood, sitting beside Myette, said, "Ask and you shall receive." Today, Cécile thinks that to this there should be added, "Give and you shall receive." But then, must everything really be begun anew and learned anew?

After ten years of marriage she still needs to learn to love.

That is to say, she must forget these physical movements for which she is gifted, and first learn the meaning of these movements, their only reason.

But with Maurice this had become impossible. The name of Maurice can no longer arouse in her anything but disgust and revolt. It is associated with too many painful and sordid memories.

She has gone the wrong way under the wrong banner.

She is nothing more, then, than a little dancer, hidden behind her makeup, applauded by the nightclub crowd, and at the casinos, and on the tours of the provinces.

She is not even protected by the glory of a Martha Graham or a Katherine Dunham.

Only one more dancer that nature has provided with charming small breasts.

PARIS SLEEPS LIKE a woman. Cécile, still dressed in gauze and painted for her act, comes home in a taxi at two in the morning.

The Place de la Concorde scarcely breathes, but a touch of distant sea air passes across it, the air that flows at this nocturnal hour.

Cécile leans her head out the window and her nostrils tremble with pleasure.

This then remains to her, in spite of everything: the pleasure of her senses, still vibrant, in search of odors, of colors, of softness to touch. This has not been taken from her like all the rest: dignity, faith, love, innocence.

It is two o'clock in the morning now, it is night, Paris sleeps, peaceful, relaxed. The taxi bumps Cécile over the large pavement stones—a Cécile all scattered in pieces, it seems to her, little pieces that she has to pick up patiently, so as to put the puzzle together again, to reconstruct an intact soul for herself.

Beneath the door, there is a white spot in the moonlight. A letter.

At once, without even reaching out her hand, Cécile knows that this letter again is from Maurice. Shall she open it, or shall she tear it up, without reading it?

She switches on the electricity, caresses her cat for a moment. It's warm in the little studio, the coal stove glows red. Cécile sits down, opens the envelope. This one begins like all the preceding letters:

I DON'T UNDERSTAND, Cécile, why you obstinately hold back from sending me even ten pages of descriptions . . . I can use no matter what . . . scenes of winter in Switzerland or summer in the Caribbean, or in Gascony, or Italy—or a little story, on any subject at all.

I know that you hate me, or believe you hate me. It is true that I often wounded you and deceived you, you were really a very innocent young girl and I have never been accustomed to virgins; besides, you went on for such a long time playing the femme fatale that I believed in it, or I, too, wanted to believe in it. To believe was so much easier for me, my little Cécile. Today, all that has passed between us has made a reunion impossible. We took too dangerous a path. Perhaps both of us play-acted for each other, each one trying to astonish the other, climbing up always higher, like acrobats on a shaking ladder, until it collapsed under our weight.

What I want to tell you, nevertheless, today, in this letter, is that you are a real writer, Cécile. This is truth. And I know about writers. You are a born writer, a natural writer, who writes the way others breathe, practically without effort; it almost seems to be play for you.

This gift—no matter what you may do to destroy your memory of me—it is I who discovered this in you, it is I who brought it to light. It is I who gave you your first weapon as a writer.

One day, Cécile, you will be famous. Yes, yes, do not smile, you will be "the famous Cécile Henry." Don't waste your life in the nightclubs. You must at once leave this profession, which is not for you. But first, make use of it, to write a novel about this profession, about this life—that, yes—and then, once the work is written, leave. Writers are vampires; they live from the blood of others, but also from their own blood. Gather the blood of the nightclubs, since chance has brought you there—then, Cécile, once the first book of your own is written, you will see, the others will follow. You will be free and you will find the happiness that I have never given you . . . happiness and glory, too, Cécile . . . glory . . .

The sheet trembles in Cécile hand.

Maurice has surrendered his arms. Maurice has admitted that she is truly a writer. Maurice, who has so often repeated to her that without him, no one, no editor would want to publish what she wrote! Now this same Maurice tells her, "Write, write by yourself, you will be famous one day."

It is as though he had a sorcerer's powers, the power to cast a spell over her one day, and now the spell is lifted.

For the first time in ten years, Cécile feels herself absolutely free, absolutely happy, as though she had just been reborn.

But is her telling the truth—this Maurice to whom it has always been so natural to lie? Or does he still want to reach Cécile in some way, to hold her by the same last device? By using praise now, as he once made use of threats, so as to get her to write a new book?

She will never know.

Slowly she gets up. A strange emotion pervades her entirely.

In the little empty studio, in the night, seated before the table in the lamplight in her dancing costume, Cécile draws a sheet of paper toward her.

They were there, the white sheets; they were waiting. Cécile takes up the pen.

A tear forms in the corner of her eye, but it does not fall, it only fogs her sight a little, and colors her eyes blue, while her pen hurries by itself, it seems, over the paper . . .

. . . Ariane is in a taxi with her husband, it is night, but there is a suffocating heat. Yesterday they were in Paris and the rain fell in torrents, it was cold, it was winter. Today they are in Bangkok, just for three days.

"You know," he says, "there are still some brothels here . . ."

"Yes, I'd like to . . ." she says.

To go to a brothel with him, like a man, to have the experience of a man, to show him that she is not afraid, that nothing can shock her . . .

He smiles. "I knew you would like the idea."

They are now before a high wall, with masses of multicolored flowers overflowing if from all sides, the heat is humid, sensual . . .

Ariane trembles, nevertheless, as though she were cold. What takes place behind that wall?

A barefooted woman opens the door; she is dressed in a Chinese gown, and her thick black hair falls down her back. Her Asiatic face is strange, enigmatic. She shows neither surprise, nor worry, nor pleasure.

Ariane and Pierre follow the woman in silence, in silence as far as another door which opens on a large room illuminated by a violent electric bulb. The room is completely white, completely bare—like an interrogation room in a detective novel. Ariane looks around her.

There is only a small table in the center of the room; behind the table sits a woman, smiling. Around the walls of the room there are benches, and on them sit some twenty young girls, a number them wearing Siamese sarongs, others in European dresses. They sit there like good schoolchildren, they are all so young—there are some very pretty ones, and some less pretty, but all of them have the tint of ancient ivory, the eyes of cats, and fragile-boned wrists. On the wall behind the young woman who smiles there is a color photo of the King of Thailand.

"Which one do you want?" says Pierre.

Is everybody then in agreement? The woman who smiles, and Pierre, and the young girls who are selling themselves— they all know that Ariane is that sort of woman—a woman so modern that she is ready to experience everything. Like Eve on the first day, reaching her hand toward the tree of Knowledge of Good and Evil—toward the apple. Just so, Ariane reaches her hand toward the round, golden face of a girl, a little Siamese of perhaps fifteen, dressed in white silk pantaloons and a black blouse with a Chinese collar . . .

Cécile stops herself for a moment. Once more then it is Maurice who has pushed her to this table, to the white sheets and the pen, and who has told her, "Quick, my little one, quick—write . . ."

Cécile smiles. It is true, it is Maurice, but now it is she alone who will write the title page.

Cécile takes another sheet of paper and slowly, she inscribes the words.

The Learning Days
by Cécile

By Cécile. . . .